ENCHANTED BY HER

CHELSEA M. CAMERON

Get Free Books and Stories!

Tropetastic romance with a twist, Happily Ever Afters guaranteed! You can expect humor and heart in every Chelsea M. Cameron romance.

Get access to a free book, free stories, and free bonus chapters! Join Chelsea's Newsletter to find out how Paige and Esme's wedding went, receive a free ebook, get access to future exclusive bonus material, news, and discounts.

And now, back to Enchanted By Her…

About Enchanted By Her

I was NOT looking forward to my sister's wedding in the fall. It's just another reminder of how single I am and how much pressure my family is putting on me to "find the one." Don't get me wrong, I'm a hopeless romantic, but all their meddling is making me feel a little murderous.

Then one day a woman walks into the bookshop where I work. She's got a sleeve of tattoos, an undercut, and a smile that makes me want to swoon. Overcome by her hotness, I blurt out a proposal: how would she like to come with me to a wedding and pretend to be my girlfriend?

Turns out Ezra Evans is new to Arrowbridge and she'll do it, but not for free. We shake on it and then I have my very own fake girlfriend and no idea what to do with her. Ezra seems to have plenty of suggestions, many of which make me blush. Things between us heat up even more before the wedding, and I can't stop wondering if this relationship might be something real after all.

Chapter One

"Mom, I'm at work," I said as I answered the phone. I had told her one thousand times to just send me a text message if she needed something, but she always ignored me, as usual. As her youngest, I might be a legal adult, but I was still her baby.

"I know, Joy, but Anna really needs to know if you're bringing a date. She's doing the seating chart on her lunch break," Mom said.

I leaned my forehead against the bookshelf in front of me. I was supposed to be tidying up the shelves, but instead I was fighting with my family again. This argument had been going for weeks, months, even.

Ever since my sister Anna had gotten engaged to her fiancé, Robert, she, my other two older sisters, and my mom, had been breathing down my neck to bring a date.

In their minds, I was poor, single Joy, and if only I was in a committed relationship, I would be happy and they could stop worrying about me dying alone. It didn't matter if I pointed out that I had two incredible best friends and a job that I loved and a book club I helped run.

Nope, none of that mattered because I didn't have a ring

on my finger or a woman on my arm. They were all happily married and they wanted me to have that, too.

It wasn't that I didn't want to be in a relationship. I wanted it more than anything. My romance-novel habit had definitely affected my views on romance, and I would love nothing more than to be with someone.

Anytime she wanted to show up, I was ready for her.

"Yes, I have a date," I blurted out, because I was out of patience. If it would get them off my back, I'd say I had a date and worry about the details later.

"You do?" Mom said so loudly that I'm sure everyone in the bookshop, Mainely Books, could hear her.

"Yes," I said, trying to inject my voice with confidence.

I didn't lie to my family. Ever. I just wasn't good at it. I felt too guilty.

This was going to be a challenge.

"Oh Joy, that's wonderful. Well, I can't wait to meet her. I have to go because my break is over, but you call me later and tell me all about it." She hung up before I could say goodbye.

"Fuck," I breathed as I leaned against the shelf again. I should call my mother back and tell her that I'd lied. The guilt was already churning in my stomach like a bad burrito.

Someone tapped me on the shoulder and I looked up to find my boss, Kendra, standing next to me.

"Sorry, sorry. If I didn't answer, she would have blown up my phone," I said, and she just shook her head as she smiled.

"Don't even worry about it. You know how my mom is," she said. Kendra's parents lived in Boston, but she talked to her mom at least once a day and they came up and visited often, so she understood what it was like to be close with your parents.

"I'm not busting you. I just wanted to let you know I'm doing a coffee run and see if you wanted a latte," she said. Kendra and I were the same age and it was nice having a boss that you could also be friends with.

"Yes, please," I said.

"Caramel?" she asked, and I nodded.

"Be right back."

Kendra left and I finished the shelves I was working on as the bell over the door dinged again, announcing a new customer. I turned to offer whomever it was a bright smile and had the breath knocked out of me instead.

The newcomer hadn't seen me yet. She had dark-brown hair that was long on top, and the sides and back were shaved into an undercut. My eyes traveled across her face, which was somewhat obscured by a pair of sunglasses, and flicked next to her right arm, which was almost entirely covered in colorful tattoos. She raised one hand to take her glasses off and I caught a glimpse of knuckle tattoos, but I couldn't make out what they were.

"Can I help you?" I asked, my voice loud in the shop. The customer swiveled toward my voice and smiled.

"Not right now, but I'll let you know," she said, her voice deep and slightly rusty. She hooked her sunglasses on the collar of her T-shirt and walked further into the space as I tried to remember how to get oxygen in and out of my lungs.

I pretended to be working on the shelf that I'd just fixed so I could calm myself down. You'd think with plenty of queer people living in Arrowbridge that I would be used to seeing beautiful women all the time, but this one hit me like a truck.

My friend Layne's type, we'd discovered, was "hot and mean," exemplified by her girlfriend Honor that she was completely in love with. My other best friend, Sydney's type was "big tits, low inhibitions."

My type? Tattoos, a hint of danger, and an edge of excitement.

Everyone called me the sweet girl, the nice girl. The little sister, the friend, the safe one.

Sometimes I got tired of it.

Finally, I peeled myself away from the shelf and walked around, pretending I was doing something booksellery, but I was really just tracking the customer. The door opened and the family that had been in the shop with us left without buying anything, so it was just me and the hot customer. I went back to the counter and fiddled on the computer as she browsed. I'd told her she could ask me if she needed any help, and I didn't want to annoy her out of the shop, so I kept my mouth shut and pretended to be busy.

She disappeared into our romance section and I cheered internally. If she wanted any recommendations, I was ready to pile her arms with books.

As I pretended I wasn't watching her every move, she pulled out three titles and then approached me.

"I'll take these," she said, setting the books down.

"Great," I said. "Did you find what you were looking for?"

My fingers trembled as I turned the books over to scan them.

"I'm not sure. I'll find out when I read them," she said, pulling a card out of the back pocket of her jeans.

"You didn't read the blurbs on the back?" I asked, knowing that she hadn't because I'd been watching her.

"Sometimes I like to be surprised. Life can be too predictable sometimes, don't you think?" she asked, turning her head slightly to the side. She tapped her card to pay and I read the letters inked on her knuckles. LOVE, with the O as a heart instead of a circle.

"I do," I said. "Are you just visiting Arrowbridge?"

It took a few tries for me to get the three books into the paper bag with the Mainely Books bookmark and the receipt.

"No, I just moved here, actually. A whole new adventure," she said, taking the bag from me.

Before I could lose my nerve, I had one more question for her.

"How would you like to go to a wedding?"

"A wedding?" she asked, and I brushed my sweaty palms on my skirt.

"A wedding," I repeated.

"Yours?" she asked, one corner of her mouth tipping up. That kind of smile could destroy me, but I couldn't get distracted. I had a mission and the universe had dropped this opportunity in my lap.

"No, my sister's. It's near the end of October." I willed my voice not to shake, and for me not to lose my nerve. If only I could become someone else, or even just a more confident Joy.

"Where is it?" she asked.

"It's about twenty minutes away, in Redfield." Anna and Robert had wanted to keep the wedding cheap and local so they'd booked a farm in our hometown.

She raised one eyebrow. "Can I wear whatever I want?"

"Yes," I said. If she'd asked to wear one of those inflatable dino suits, I would have said yes. Hell, if she wanted to show up naked, I'd say yes.

And now I was picturing her naked. I wondered just how many tattoos she had…

"Weddings are expensive. I'll need an outfit and money for travel and new shoes, of course. Hmmm, let's see… I'll do it for a thousand bucks," she said, and it took me a minute for her words to make sense.

This stranger was agreeing to go to my sister's wedding after talking to me for five minutes, but she wanted a thousand dollars to do it?

"What's your name?" I asked, even though I could have just read it off her card when she paid.

"Ezra," she said, holding out the hand with the knuckle tattoos. "Nice to meet you…" she trailed off waiting for me to answer. This was not the first time that I was grateful that my boss, Kendra, didn't make us wear nametags.

"Joy," I said. "I'm Joy."

Ezra shook my hand with warm, strong fingers that were just a little bit rough. I wondered what activity had made those hands rough. And what else she could do with such strong fingers.

Focus, Joy. Shut those hormones down. Get back to business.

"Joy," she repeated, smiling as she said it. As if she liked saying it. "You certainly are."

At that moment, I cursed my tendency to blush when someone said something flirty to me. And sometimes when they didn't.

The door opened, and it was like a spell had broken. I'd completely forgotten that anyone other than me and the incredible woman in front of me existed in the world.

"A thousand?" I asked, hoping that Ezra would tell me that the number was a joke.

She lifted one shoulder. "I read an article about a woman who works as a professional bridesmaid who charges two thousand. I gave you a fifty percent discount."

My mouth dropped open. "Two thousand dollars to be a fake bridesmaid? Are you serious?" I was in the wrong line of work.

"You can make a career out of anything if you believe hard enough and can find people to pay you," Ezra said. "I'm in. Are you?"

A flicker of doubt went through me. Why was this stranger agreeing to do this without having any other questions? I know if I were in her shoes, I'd want to know all the details before jumping in.

Maybe that was why I was perpetually single. I always had to know the details before saying yes to something.

"Let me think about it," I said. Confident, bold Joy was gone. Regular, cautious Joy had returned. Probably a silly idea to try and change the personality I'd had for twenty-six years.

Something flickered through Ezra's eyes. People would probably call the color hazel, but it was such a boring word for eyes so unusual and magnetic. All those colors swirling together like a kaleidoscope.

"Okay, Joy," she said. There was something indecent about the way she said my name. It made me think dirty thoughts. "Thanks for the books."

She took the bag and winked at me before I could remember that I didn't have any way of contacting her. I dashed around the counter and looked out the door, glancing up and down Main Street of Arrowbridge, Maine. The sidewalk was packed with people enjoying their summer Friday.

Where could she have gone? I squinted, trying to see that dark head of hair or that arm of tattoos, but she'd vanished. Short of abandoning the bookstore and searching through every other shop, I was out of luck.

I went back inside the bookshop and sighed. So much for that. I'd probably never see her again.

Chapter Two

"What's wrong?" Sydney, my roommate asked the minute I walked into our apartment, conveniently located right above the bookshop.

"You will not believe what happened to me today," I said, setting my bag down and slipping off my shoes.

Clementine, Sydney's cat, ran over to rub against my legs and meow at me that he hadn't been fed yet.

"Poor kitty," I said, leaning down to pet him as he made the most pitiful sounds of a starving creature before rolling onto the floor and staring up at me.

"He literally just ate," Sydney said, shaking her head at the dramatics.

"I figured," I said, walking over to the kitchen where Sydney was seated on one of the stools at the counter that separated the kitchen and the living room. I slid onto the stool beside her and sighed.

"You want me to cook tonight?" she asked.

"No, it's fine, I've got it."

Syd and I switched off who cooked, but we both knew that I had more skill than she did, so most nights I would make enough so we could eat leftovers the next day and all she'd have to do is heat up a plate when she came upstairs for lunch.

Sydney tucked one of her dark-brown curls behind her ear. "So? You going to tell me how your day was?"

"You wouldn't believe me if I told you," I said, getting up. If I didn't start dinner now, I was going to sit for too long and lose the energy.

I pulled some chicken out of the fridge as well as some peppers and onions for fajitas.

"The suspense is killing me," Syd said, practically draping herself on the counter. "Come on, I need some excitement. I'm dying here."

As I chopped peppers and got the chicken in a pan, I told Sydney about my encounter with the stranger named Ezra.

"Have you seen her around?" I asked.

"A gorgeous woman with knuckle tattoos? No, I think I'd remember that," Sydney said. "She doesn't really sound like the kind of person who would buy pottery anyway."

Sydney managed the pottery store her mother owned. Unfortunately, Sydney had not inherited her mother's talent with pottery, but her skills at business and marketing and organizing the shop had transformed the shop since she'd taken over for her mother. Still, being an only child meant Sydney carried the disappointment of her mother's dreams of being a mother-daughter pottery duo.

"Maybe I just imagined her. I mean, she literally disappeared." I flipped the chicken and then added the peppers and onions to cook. Joy got out plates and the bowl of leftover cucumber and tomato salad we had for a side.

"What possessed you to ask her to come to your sister's wedding? That is so un-Joy-like," Sydney said, but I could tell she was impressed. Sydney was always telling me to take more risks and be more outgoing. Well, there wasn't much more outgoing you could get than asking a stranger to come to a wedding with you.

"I have no idea," I said. "I think she was just so hot that I didn't even know what I was saying."

Sydney laughed as I dished up my fajitas and moved aside so she could make hers up.

"Well, whatever it was, I like it," she said, lightly bumping my hip with hers.

"She wants a thousand dollars to do it, Syd. That feels…weird."

Sydney shrugged. "You have to respect the hustle. People are creating all kinds of strange jobs now. There are professional cuddlers. Sugar babies. Hell, it can't be worse than trading imaginary money on the internet."

She did have a point there.

I shook my head. "It doesn't even matter because she probably wasn't serious. I bet that's why she asked for that much money. Because who would pay that?"

Sydney gave me a smirk. "How hot was she?"

I closed my eyes and conjured Ezra in my mind. "So hot, Syd. So freaking hot."

∼

SYDNEY and I headed to the neighboring town of Castleton on Saturday to take advantage of an unexpected heat wave and get in some sun and sand and surf with our other best friend, Layne and her girlfriend, Honor.

"They're so happy, it makes me sick," Sydney said as we got out of the car and waved to Layne and Honor. They were a mis-matched couple, at least when you first saw them.

Layne wore a pair of ripped jean shorts that she had made out of an old pair of jeans herself, along with a tank top she'd bought at the bookstore.

Enchanted By Her

Honor wore a white linen jumpsuit with a black bathing suit underneath, designer sunglasses, and a black hat.

Everything about Honor screamed "classy." Not that Layne wasn't, but that wasn't the first word you'd associate with her, that was for sure. I loved her, but it was true.

"You're just jealous," I said to Sydney and she glared at me. That was true too. Sydney could go on and on about how she didn't want a relationship, she just wanted meaningless sex, but we both knew she was full of shit. One of these days she was going to get hit in the face by love and it was going to knock her off her feet.

I couldn't wait to see it.

Sydney yanked her sunglasses off her head and shoved them on her face.

"I'm definitely not. The only thing I feel right now is nausea."

"Cheer up, my dear. We don't have to do any work for the entire day."

That made Syd smile. "A day with no pottery."

My day wasn't going to be without books, but at least I didn't have to unpack them, or deal with any annoying customers.

"Ready?" Layne said as she pulled out her folding chairs from the back of Honor's car.

She might look like someone who was stressed about breaking an acrylic, but Honor took charge of the cooler and one of the beach chairs while Layne wrestled with the other chair and an umbrella. Sydney stepped in and hoisted the umbrella over her shoulder, which was a task, because Syd did not pack light. At all.

I used to joke that she needed more equipment than an actual baby. Today she'd brought a whole tent to shield herself from the sun, as well as four different kinds of sunscreen, three pairs of sunglasses, three books (one non-fiction, our current book club book, and a cozy mystery from her favorite author), two pairs of shoes, an entire bag of snacks, and so much else, only some of it useful.

Sydney might have a lot of shit, but Layne was the one who brought bottles of aloe lotion for potential sunburns and a first aid kit in case anyone cut their feet on a shell.

Layne was always prepared for emergencies, and I think it was what made her such a good nanny to the twins that she took care of.

"Riley and Zoey would like you all to know they are upset they weren't invited, so you're both going to have to make an appearance at their sleepover in two weeks," Layne said as she huffed and puffed her stuff toward the ticket booth where we flashed our passes and then down to the sand.

"I'll be there," I told her, laughing. Riley and Zoey were eleven, and just on the cusp of becoming surly teens who thought all adults were uncool, so I was going to enjoy my cool factor as long as it lasted.

"Me too. Love those kids," Sydney said. "I don't like a lot of kids, but they're fun. I can't wait until they get old enough to make really bad decisions."

Layne stopped walking and gave Syd a glare. "I'm going to pretend I didn't hear that."

"Oh come on. I've made lots of bad decisions and I've turned out fine."

Layne and I gave her a look.

"Mostly fine," she amended.

The four of us parked ourselves on a bit of sand and set up our chairs and umbrella and Sydney put up her tent surprisingly fast.

"It's a skill," she said.

"And yet you wouldn't be caught dead camping," Layne said.

Sydney shuddered. "I'm allergic to camping."

"What are your feelings on the institution of camping?" Layne asked Honor, who was deep in a celebrity hardback biography she'd gotten from the library.

"I'd go camping with you," she said, not looking up from her page.

"You would?" Layne asked. Honor glanced up and smiled. Honor was one of those people who looked like they were living in the wrong era. She definitely belonged in the pages of a vintage fashion magazine, or in the golden age of Hollywood as a movie star, flashbulbs going off every time she got out of a car.

"Of course. I'd go anywhere with you," Honor said, stroking Layne's arm as Layne blushed and giggled. I stopped myself from letting out a little sigh at how cute they were. Sydney didn't hold back the little grumble from the shade of her tent.

"Okay, but what kind of camping?" Layne asked. "Would you go camping with me to a place with no electricity, no bathroom, and no sign of civilization for miles?"

Honor thought about that. "Is that a challenge?"

"No, I'm just curious."

That started a conversation about what level of camping we could tolerate.

"I think I could rough it," Layne said. "I'm not super confident in my ability to catch a fish with no supplies, but I think I could start a fire. I chaperoned a few of the twins scout meetings when they were into it and I like to think that some of the skills rubbed off on me."

"I'm not shitting in the woods," Sydney announced.

"Thank you, I'm so glad we all know that now," I said as Honor made a choking noise. Sometimes I thought that we were too much for her, but she didn't complain.

"I think I could do mid-level," I said. "Where it's kind of in the wilderness, but there's a town a few minutes away with supplies in case anything goes wrong."

"I thought about going on one of those shows where they drop you in the middle of nowhere with nothing and then film you trying to survive," Honor said.

"Oh my god, I love those shows," Sydney said. "I'm happy to watch other people struggle from the comfort of my own couch."

"You would not," Layne said to Honor. "I cannot picture it. Your hair would probably still be perfect, though."

Layne smoothed back Honor's hair that was already smooth.

"My hair is always perfect," Honor said.

It had taken me a little bit to get used to her confidence. When she said things like that, she meant them because they were true. There was an honesty to her that was so refreshing compared to the way I constantly tried to contort myself into a pretzel to make other people comfortable.

My mom. My sisters. Sydney and Layne (even though they would call me out if they caught me doing it).

Honor gave Layne a soft smile and asked her if she wanted to take a walk. Sydney decided she was taking a nap in her tent and I went back to reading. Even with the screaming kids and the frisbee game going on near us, the day was perfectly peaceful. I lost myself in one of my top five books. Sometimes you just needed a good comfort read. Lately I'd been needing them more and more.

A text message from my mom came in, asking for the name of my date to the wedding.

Well, shit.

Her name is Ezra. She just moved to Arrowbridge. We met at the bookstore, I sent her. None of those things was a lie. I'd just left out that Ezra hadn't agreed to be my date, the fact that if she did, I was going to have to pay her, and that we'd just met this week.

Sometimes with my mom, leaving out information was for the best for all involved.

I can't wait to meet her. You should invite her to the bridal shower, Mom sent back.

That was going to be a hell no.

She doesn't know anyone. That would probably make her really uncomfortable, I replied. The truth was, I didn't know if Ezra would be comfortable or not because I'd spent all of ten minutes with her. She was a complete stranger.

A hot, sexy stranger that made me feel things in my downstairs area that made me need to go have some alone time.

"Hey," a voice said, startling me out of my reverie. Sydney had poked her head out of her tent, her face sleepy.

"Good morning, sunshine," I said, giving her a smile.

"Hush, you," she said. "I need ice cream."

"Right now?" I asked.

Syd nodded. Now that she'd mentioned ice cream, I realized I had a craving for it as well.

I sent a quick text to Layne on the other end of the beach and asked if she wanted to join us, but she declined. Too busy trying to lull Honor into a false sense of security before trying to dump an armload of seaweed on her head.

If I didn't need ice cream, I really would have liked to see that, but right now my craving was a more pressing concern. I told Layne that she had to get pictures or video or it didn't count.

Sydney and I got in line and she couldn't decide what she wanted to get, so I had her list her top three picks and then helped her choose. Syd was pretty decisive in most areas of her life, but food was one where she could never choose.

"What are you getting?" she asked.

"Chocolate cherry in a waffle cone with sprinkles," I said. "Rainbow sprinkles."

"Oh yes, of course. They must be rainbow."

"Of course," I said, laughing.

We finally ordered at the window and then waited around the corner where the pickup window was.

Sydney cringed as a small child carried a very large tray piled high with hot dogs and fries and onion rings to a picnic table.

"A seagull is going to attack that kid, just you watch," she said.

There were multiple signs around us warning about the vicious birds that would swoop down and take food right out of your hand if you weren't careful. At least once every beach trip I heard the wail of a sad child that had their food taken from them.

"I don't enjoy the suffering of others," I said.

"I don't either, but you have to admit it's kind of funny."

Syd and I finally got our ice cream and took it back to our spot on the sand with us, guarding our treats the whole time.

My cone wasn't too melty by the time we sat down, which was nice.

I couldn't see Layne and Honor, but I assumed they were probably making out somewhere.

I was admiring the perfect amount of sprinkles on my cone when a bright voice said, "Hi, Joy!"

I looked up to find Mia, who was my boss's niece. Technically my boss's girlfriend's niece, but they were family in my book.

"Hi, Mia," I said. "Are you here with Theo and Kendra?"

Mia shook her head. She was seven and more confident than a lot of adults I knew.

"No, I'm here with Mommy and Daddy and Oliver," Mia said. "Oliver won't stop trying to eat the sand."

I bit back a smile. "Babies do things like that, don't they?"

Mia nodded. "Mommy asks me to help her watch him sometimes. I stopped him from eating a rock."

"Well, that's because you're a very responsible big sister," I said. Mia was such a fun kid, and she'd adjusted to having a baby brother surprisingly well.

"Tell your parents I said hello," I told her.

"I will, bye," she said, waving and then darting off to chase a seagull.

"She's too funny," Sydney said.

"I know. She cracks me up whenever she comes into the bookstore."

Sydney and I were finishing our ice creams when Layne and Honor came back, their fingers entwined as they whispered to each other, their heads bent together.

Seeing Layne so happy made me emotional, and I had to look away. Honor might not have been what I pictured for Layne, but she treated her like gold and she made Layne smile every day. What more could you ask for?

Now if only I could find that for myself.

Chapter Three

MONDAY CAME FAR TOO SOON, as it always did. Even though I adored my job, it was still work, and I did have to gear myself up for a new week.

"Coffee," Sydney said, as she did every morning.

"In the pot," I said as I waited for my waffles to finish warming in the air fryer.

"Can you throw a few in for me when yours are done?" Sydney said through a yawn.

"Of course."

We'd lived together for a few years now and our routine was pretty well established at this point. It was pretty convenient that we went to work at the same time.

Living with Sydney was comfortable, and I liked having someone around. Clementine yowled to be fed, and Sydney got out a can of wet food for him.

"Oh my god, you need to calm down," Sydney said as she broke up the food and then set the bowl down next to his water dish.

Clementine started chomping as if he'd never eaten in his entire life.

"He gets to eat before I do, explain that to me," Sydney said as I pulled out the waffles and set them on my plate before shoving three more in the fryer and setting the timer for her.

"He screams. Maybe you should start screaming until someone sets a bowl of food in front of you," I said.

Sydney leaned against the counter. "Do you think that would work?"

"Might get an ambulance to show up, which wouldn't really help in the food department," I said, carefully swiping butter on my waffles before adding just the right amount of syrup and cutting them into the right size pieces.

I sat on one of the stools and ate my waffles and sipped my coffee and enjoyed the noises of the morning. Mostly just Sydney humming whatever song was stuck in her head right now. Clementine finished his food and started begging me for more by tapping my leg with his paw.

"Go sit in your window. There's probably birds out there," I said. At the b word, he raced to the window that faced the street and sat on his little perch that we set next to the couch for him. Sydney had found a bird feeder that suction-cupped to the window and that was what Clementine spent the majority of his day watching. It was a hard job, but someone had to do it.

Sydney and I finished up breakfast and got our act together to head downstairs to our respective businesses.

"See you for break?" Syd said and nodded.

She saluted me. "Off to the salt mines."

I laughed and unlocked the bookstore, rushing to put in the alarm code as quickly as possible to stop the beeping. My first week here I'd set it off and had been horribly embarrassed when I had to call the company and tell them not to send the police. I'd thought for sure that Kendra would fire me, but she'd just laughed and told me it was no big deal.

She really was a great boss.

I was alone for the first fifteen minutes of my shift, but as I checked the store and made sure the bathrooms were clean, I heard a key in the lock.

"It's just me," a bright voice said.

"Good morning," I called out as I left the bathroom to find Kendra carrying two cups of coffee from the local café. I rushed to take her bag, which was falling off her shoulder.

"You are a lifesaver," I said, even though this was my second cup of the day.

"I do what I can," Kendra said. Her soft brown hair was pulled back in a clip and she wore a crisp white T-shirt with the bookstore logo on a little pocket on her chest.

"Is that the new merch?" I asked, pointing at the shirt.

"You like?" she said, gesturing at the pocket.

"I love," I said. She opened her tote bag and pulled something out.

"Well, that's good because I have one for you."

She unfurled a shirt for me, in a beautiful dark green color with a white logo.

"This is so pretty," I said. "Can I put it on right now?"

"I'd be mad if you didn't," Kendra said, pushing me toward the bathroom.

I shucked off my other shirt and pulled on the new one that Kendra had given me. It was so freaking soft and the color really worked for me. After a few checks in the mirror, I walked back out and did a little spin for Kendra.

"Gorgeous," she said as I posed a few times, feeling foolish.

"Now we just have to put them through the ultimate test of a full sweaty day, and then see how they handle the washer," Kendra said, shuddering.

We'd learned from previous mistakes to always test drive clothing before we decided to sell it. Once we'd ordered black shirts and they'd used a cheap dye that ended up staining your skin if you sweat or got the shirt wet. Complete disaster.

Fashion show over, Kendra and I went through the steps it took to open up for the day and welcome the first customers. Kendra said she needed to get some work done in the office, so I took charge of the rest of the shop, which was fine with me.

My day went by in a blur, as it usually did. The stream of customers was steady, and I was on my feet nearly the whole time. Kendra tapped me on the shoulder when it was time for my break and shoved me out the door as she took over the register.

I met Syd outside of the café and we got in line to get wraps and smoothies. We didn't do it every day, but Mondays required wraps and smoothies, with cupcakes for dessert.

"Mom's on a rampage. She was working on this special order and some of the pots got messed up in the kiln," Sydney said, sipping her smoothie. "Not going to lie, I wish this had champagne in it."

"I'm sorry. Is she blaming you?" I asked.

Syd shook her head, a few curls escaping her ponytail. "No, but I have to listen to her rant about it and make sympathetic sounds. And I'll have to bring her dinner when she stays up late to redo them."

Sydney sighed. Her burdens as an only child seemed pretty heavy to me. At least I had older sisters to shoulder a lot of the load when it came to my parents.

"Well, you don't have to make dinner tonight. I'm doing the gnocchi with veggies and sausage so you can have that for lunch tomorrow." It was one of Syd's favorite meals and pretty easy for me to make—putting everything on a baking sheet and then cooking the pasta on the stove before throwing it to crisp up just a little bit in a pan with the balsamic sauce.

"Have I told you that you're my favorite?" Sydney said, giving me an adoring look.

"Don't let Layne hear you say that. She's a better cook than I am," I said. I wasn't knocking my own skills, but Layne had much more experience from her job. She had to be a creative cook to take care of the family she worked for over all these years and keep them all fed and happy. I could outdo her with book recommendations, though, so I had that going for me.

"You're a better cook than I am," Syd grumbled.

"Yes, but you have the ability to calm an angry customer like you've put a spell on them," I said. I'd seen her in action and it was amazing to behold. Sydney had a strong personality, but she could switch on the charm and take even the grumpiest customer and turn their frown upside down.

I did my best, but when people were really upset, I got flustered and sometimes didn't know what to say to bring the situation down. It was something I was working on to be better at my job.

Sydney grinned at me. "I am really good at that, you're right."

"You're skilled at lots of things, Syd, you know that," I said. Most people only saw the brash, confident side of Syd and they didn't see her softer underbelly that she only showed to me and Layne, and sometimes her mom. Sydney's mom had a tendency to use words that sliced at those vulnerable parts of Syd, and Layne and I were always right there to pick her up and care for those wounds.

In some ways, I was closer to Layne and Syd than I was to my own sisters.

"I am, aren't I?" she said, grinning at me. There she was. I laughed and we finished our lunches before going back to work.

~

I HAD to keep ignoring calls from my mom that night and the next day. She was pestering me about wedding details and I didn't have answers for her because I hadn't seen Ezra. I'd even done a few strolls in town, checking various shops on the off chance she might be there. I even did a sweep through the grocery store.

If I truly wanted to know about Ezra, I could have gone over to talk to Sadie at Rizo, a sweet little boutique a few doors down from the bookshop. It was run by one of Layne's bosses, but she was more like a friend than an employer, like me and Kendra.

Sadie liked to keep her ear to the ground on what was going on, though no one would ever accuse her of being a gossip. She just happened to know everything that was going on in Arrowbridge at all times. On the flipside, if you had a secret and you wanted someone to keep it for you? Sadie was the woman for the job.

Part of me didn't want to say anything to Sadie because then she'd want to know why I was asking about someone I'd talked to for just a few minutes and I had a bad habit of blurting things out when given a little pushback, so no doubt I'd spill the whole thing and that would be beyond embarrassing. Layne, Honor, and Sydney already knew far too much about me. I'd like to at least try and keep some things private.

If only the universe would do me a favor and drop Ezra back into my world so I could figure out my next steps. Telling my mom and sister that I didn't have a date for the wedding, that my plan had fallen through, would suck, and I wanted to put that off as long as possible and try and find an Ezra alternative.

My last-resort plan was to take Sydney. We'd have fun, but I also didn't want to field all the questions about our relationship and if we were dating, and explaining that we were just roommates, no not because we were afraid to come out, we were really just friends…

It got exhausting fending off the same questions over and over. Sydney had come with me to one of my other sister's bridal showers and it had been a whole thing. No one in my family knew how to mind their business, or what appropriate questions were.

I thought of Ezra and her confidence. She wouldn't put up with that shit. Or she'd have the perfect response ready, while I flailed and looked for a chance to run away.

For someone else, taking Sydney seemed like it would be no big deal, but I just… Was I so undesirable that I couldn't find a single date? Were my prospects that bleak?

Then a voice in my head would remind me that I was contemplating paying someone to be my date, so was I really all that concerned about romance?

Those cheery thoughts were my companion as I emptied the bathroom trash can and then washed my hands before doing my sweep of the shop. Kendra was in the back with Theo unloading boxes and I was a little upset that I couldn't be there to watch the show.

Theo unloading boxes was a sight to behold if you had any sapphic leanings. Kendra was a lucky, lucky woman.

No doubt they were lightly bickering about the best way to unpack the boxes and then stealing kisses since they knew no one was looking.

I wanted that. I wanted it so much that there was a constant ache in my chest.

Someone had clearly put some books back in the wrong place when they decided not to buy them, so I went to work fixing the mistake someone else had made.

I was concentrating and didn't hear someone come up behind me until there was a tap on my shoulder. I jumped, dropping two paperbacks with blue aliens and human women on the covers.

"Crap," I said, leaning down to pick up the books. A tattooed hand darted in front of mine, seizing one of the paperbacks.

"I didn't mean to startle you," a rich voice said, and I looked up from the books to meet Ezra's kaleidoscope eyes. Her lashes were long and dark, and I wondered if they were extensions or just really good mascara.

Ezra handed me the book and our fingers brushed. There was that zing of something again. I'd never felt someone's touch quite like that before.

I realized we were both still crouched on the floor and stood up with the two books. What had I been doing with these? I couldn't even remember.

"It's okay," I finally said to Ezra.

"Are you busy?" she asked, and I looked at the books in my hands, struggling to remember where they needed to go.

"No, I'm not busy," I said automatically, cringing at how eager my voice sounded in my ears. Ugh.

"Great. Well, I wanted to see if you'd made a decision about our potential arrangement."

How did she make all of those words sound dirty?

"Oh, uh," I said, looking around. I didn't exactly want to discuss this in the store where people could hear. We weren't alone. There were quite a few people wandering the shelves.

"We can meet for coffee later, if now isn't a good time," Ezra said, sensing my reluctance.

"That might be good," I said. "I get off at five-thirty."

"Perfect. I'll see you then," she said, and I thought she was going to say something else, but she didn't. She just smiled in that way that made my stomach do a flip and walked out without buying a book.

∼

SOMEHOW I GOT through the rest of my day, but Kendra noticed that I wasn't completely there.

"Sorry, I'm a little distracted," I said, when I had to restart counting the cash in the register for the second time. Most of our transactions were via credit card, but sometimes a kid would come in with their birthday money for the comic book they'd been wanting, or an older customer would want to buy a knitting book with cash.

"Hey, how about you take off and let me deal with this?" Kendra said. Theo was in the back taking care of the last of the boxes.

"Are you sure?" I asked and she bumped her shoulder against mine.

"I'm sure. Get out of here."

That meant that I was sitting at a table at the café down the street fifteen minutes early, one of my crossed legs jiggling against the other.

I wasn't very good at being patient, or hiding my stress, but I was doing my best.

Could I do this? Spend a thousand dollars on a wedding date?

I imagined what my mother would say if I told her that I hadn't found a date. That it had fallen through. I could just hear the disappointment in her voice. My sister Anna would be upset about her seating chart. And then there would be the wedding itself. All those questions about when I was going to find someone to settle down with.

My stomach rolled in an unpleasant way and my palms started sweating. No, I couldn't endure it. I'd rather have multiple root canals than have to manage all that while trying not to trip in my shoes or spill anything on my dress.

No, I'd deal with the loss of the money if it could save me from all that. It didn't hurt at all that Ezra was…well. She was hot as hell. There was no better way to put it. She was stunning and sexy and in our limited interactions, she looked like a woman who could hold her own. Unlike me.

When I pictured Ezra with me at the wedding, a calm came over me. Like the first sip of cold lemonade on a hot day.

Even though I still had some time to wait, the door opened and in walked Ezra. I held my breath for a second as she scanned the space, her eyes locking on mine as she smiled slowly. As if she was happy to see me.

Ezra walked over and pulled out the other chair, sitting down carefully.

"Hi," I said.

"I'm not usually early, but I see you beat me," she said. Her outfit looked ripped from a fall queer fashion social media account. I had no idea where she got her clothes, but I wanted to know.

"Sorry," I said, apologizing instantly.

Ezra shook her head. "It's okay. You don't have to apologize. Should we get some coffee first?"

I nodded, even though I didn't need any caffeine right now. Ezra moved aside so I could get ahead of her in line.

"What's good here?" she asked, leaning down and speaking in my ear. Her breath was warm on my skin.

"Oh, um," I said, suddenly forgetting everything I'd ever had at this café, and then losing the ability to read the menu board.

I blinked a few times and took a deep breath, hoping Ezra didn't notice how much she had affected me.

I was going to have to get over my reactions to her if I was going to get through all this wedding nonsense.

"I always get a caramel macchiato and a cherry danish. Boring, I know," I said. Something about Ezra made me blurt out everything I didn't want her to know.

"That doesn't sound boring," she said. "But I'm more of halva honey latte and almond croissant kind of woman."

"That sounds good too," I said even though I didn't really

know what a halva latte was. I'd seen it on the menu, but I'd never been brave enough to try it.

We got our respective orders and Ezra said to put my order on her card.

"It's the least I can do if you're going to be paying me to be your date," she said, her voice low enough that only I could hear.

"That seems fair," I said as we waited for our orders and then carried them back to our table.

"So," Ezra said, sipping her latte, not getting any foam on her lip, "are we doing this?"

I looked into my cup and then back up at her. "I mean, do you still want to?"

Ezra leaned back in her chair, her eyes flicking up and down my body in a way that made my cheeks go red.

"I'm in if you are," she said.

Without considering or thinking it over, I spoke.

"I'm in."

Ezra smiled, and I noted that just one of her teeth was chipped. A small imperfection that only made her more attractive.

"Then let's hammer out some details."

I picked up my coffee, my hands finally steady.

˜

"HAMMERING OUT DETAILS" turned out to be a lot more fun than I thought it was going to be.

"So what kind of wedding are we talking about here?" Ezra asked, taking a bite of croissant. "Since it's in October, I'm guessing spooky?"

I laughed. "Actually, no. Anna is very anti when it comes to spooky. She was going for more of a harvest fall vibe."

"So that's going to be a no on wearing anything with skeletons on it?" Ezra asked.

For a moment, I imagined Ezra showing up in a skeleton outfit and the sheer horror on my sister's face.

"Yeah, that's a definite no. The bridesmaid's dresses are all varying shades of red and bronze and gold."

"I'm sure you'll look lovely in any of them," Ezra said, making me blush again.

"What should I wear?" Ezra asked after a moment of silence while I tried to collect myself.

"You can wear what you want, as far as I'm concerned."

"But no skeletons," she said.

"Right, no skeletons."

"What I mean, is that if I wear a suit, will there be an issue?"

Ezra wasn't just asking about clothes. She was asking if my family would be cool with her showing up the way she wanted to present.

"My family would be fine with you wearing a suit," I said.

Ezra nodded. "Good. Because while I have worn dresses in the past, they're not exactly the most comfortable. A suit is more my style."

"I think you'd look great in a suit," I said before I could stop myself. Ezra wouldn't just look great in a suit. She'd look incredible.

"Why thank you, Joy," she said. Our coffees and pastries had been finished and I needed to get back home to make dinner, but I didn't want to end this meeting.

We still hadn't talked about the money, and I was avoiding bringing it up. Things always seemed to get complicated when you added money to the equation.

"So, you need me for the bridal shower, the rehearsal dinner, and the wedding? What about the bachelorette?" Ezra asked.

"I can handle the bachelorette on my own," I said. Anna decided instead of going out, she wanted a more lowkey bachelorette, so her best friend and maid of honor, Eliza, had rented a beautiful cabin by a lake for the weekend. It might be chilly, but Anna was excited about doing a hike or something and getting cozy by the fire and watching movies. Out of all of my sisters, Anna was the most chill, but then she could turn on a dime if something disrupted her chill. Like me not having a date to her wedding so she couldn't finalize everything.

"Fair enough," Ezra said, nodding and then seemed to be waiting for me to say something. We seemed to have arrived at the "money" step of the negotiation. Everything about this part made me feel gross, but she was the one who had suggested money and if she was going to do this, that was her price.

"I can just send it to you," I said, pulling out my phone.

"How about this? You send me one-third now, then the second after the bridal shower, then the next after the wedding? You know, to keep me honest."

That last word gave me pause. "Are you ever dishonest?" I asked.

Ezra smiled that way that made me feel warm inside. "Rarely."

"Are you being honest with me?" I asked.

"Only one way to find out. You're the one who approached me."

There was no way to argue with that.

"Who," I said, my mouth suddenly dry, "who do I send it to?"

Ezra gave me her email address and I pulled up the app to send exactly three hundred and thirty-three dollars and thirty-three cents to the email that she'd given me. I had to type in the numbers twice when my fingers shook.

My phone made a whooshing sound as the money sent and

a second later, Ezra's phone signaled a new notification.

"It's been a pleasure doing business with you, Joy. A pleasure." Ezra stood up and held her hand out to shake mine. I shook and then she turned around to leave.

"You can send the details to that same email address," she said over her shoulder as she walked out of the café.

What the hell had I just gotten myself into?

∼

"YOU DID WHAT?!" Sydney said, when I told her that I'd paid Ezra the first third of the money to be my wedding date.

"I paid her."

"Yeah, and what's to say she's not going to just disappear now?" Sydney said. "Joy, I swear to god, you trust people way too easily."

It wasn't that I trusted people too easily. I guess I just saw the good in them when others might not. I gave the benefit of the doubt. That didn't mean I would let just anyone in. When it came to letting people see me, the real me, there were only a few who I trusted with that Joy. Everyone else got smiling, helpful, sweet Joy. Everyone liked that Joy, which was the point.

"If she goes with me to the events, she gets more money, so she has an incentive to stay. I just paid her an advance," I said.

Sydney looked at me as if I'd announced that I was moving out and joining the circus.

"An advance," she said.

"Yes, an advance."

She shook her head and went back to the stove, where she stirred a big pan of fried rice.

"I think this is going to blow up in your face, Joy, but you're an adult and I'm not going to stop you. I might say 'I told you so,' but I'll be nice about it."

"No, you wouldn't," I said.

She sighed as I got out some plates. "You act like I want this to fail, but I don't. I just don't want you to get your hopes up and then have someone hurt you."

I wrapped my arm around her and gave her shoulders a squeeze.

"I know. I feel the same way about you. But this isn't that big of a deal. It's not going to ruin my life."

Sydney looked down at me and I could see a flicker of worry cross her face.

"I wish I had your confidence," she said.

~

I SENT Ezra the details of the bridal shower and the wedding later that night. As much as I'd put on a brave face in front of Sydney, the seeds of doubt were starting to grow. What if I'd just handed off three hundred dollars to a total scammer? She was charming and gorgeous enough to be a scammer. Plus, she had been the one who brought up payment.

Was I getting taken for a ride?

I set my phone on my bedside table and tried to go to sleep, but it wasn't happening, so I grabbed my e-reader and pulled up my favorite comfort book. It was a romance between enemy time-travelers and I'd already read it a dozen times, but it was so beautiful that I found something new every time I perused it again.

I had just gotten sucked into the story when my phone went off. I'd forgotten to turn off the notifications for the night.

Ezra had answered my email.

You didn't mention that the shower is themed. Now I have to pick which flannel shirt works best for the "Falling in Love" theme.

It was hard to tell with emails, but I was ninety-nine percent sure she was joking. I typed a response.

You could always send me some options. I'm happy to assist in any way I can.

Her response came about a minute later. I wondered if Ezra was a night owl, like me.

You're just fishing so I'll send you pictures.

I snorted and typed out a reply.

Is it working?

I could almost hear the chuckle in her response.

I'll let you know tomorrow. Goodnight, Joy.

Not sure if I should respond to that, I just let the thread drop and went back to my book.

Chapter Four

LAYNE CAME to visit me the next day for lunch, and I got to have her take on the whole situation. Her predictions weren't as dire as Syd's, but she still didn't foresee any way of this going well.

"I would have gone with you to the wedding," she said. "I don't think Honor would mind."

I snorted. "Honor would definitely mind."

Layne thought about that as she chewed her sandwich.

"Okay, she probably would mind, but I could deal with that. What do you even know about this person?"

I couldn't lie and say that I knew a lot, because I really didn't.

"I just have a feeling about her," I said.

"So you're going on vibes," Layne said. "What if your vibes turn out to be wrong?"

"Then I have a great story," I said. "Honestly, I think everyone is making a big deal about this. Other people have hired dates for weddings. It's a whole industry. Some people do it as a job." I pulled up the article I'd found on one of the best-known "professional bridesmaids" and showed it to Layne.

"She gets paid how much? Damn, I am in the wrong line of work." She finished the article and handed my phone back.

"Layne, you love your job," I said.

"Fine, I do. But I wouldn't mind getting paid bank to attend a bunch of weddings. Although, it might be kind of stressful. I'll take caring for twins any day."

I couldn't decide what would be more stressful: caring for twins or caring for a stressed-out bride. Both sounded like a nightmare. I loved kids, adored my nieces and nephew, but being tasked with their wellbeing was way too much responsibility. I'd much rather show up with some books and puzzles and toys and be Auntie Joy and leave the doctor's appointments and feeding and sleep schedules to their parents.

"What's her name again?" Layne asked.

"Ezra Evans," I said. I'd only found out her last name when I'd sent her the payment.

"Ezra Evans," Layne said. "I'll see what I can find out."

"No, don't," I said. "You don't have to do that."

Layne gave me a look. "Do you not want me to investigate her because you're scared she's a con artist?"

"How can she be a con artist when I was the one who approached her?" I said, stabbing at a tomato in my salad.

"But she was the one who asked about money." I was so tired of this conversation.

"She wants to be paid for her time, what's wrong with that?"

Layne opened her mouth to argue, but then she couldn't.

"Fine. I won't go digging. But if I hear anything shady, I'm going to tell you. I just want my best friend to be safe," Layne said.

That's what Syd had said too. I loved my friends, but sometimes they were too much. I wasn't some naive child that needed to be shielded from the world.

"I know," I said. "But can you trust me to trust my own instincts?"

Layne nodded immediately. "Of course. Of course. Though I feel the need to point out that you didn't exactly trust me about Honor when we started seeing each other."

"Because you didn't trust her when you first met her either!" I said. "Syd and I were just going off what you told us about her!"

Layne made a few nonsensical noises before she could form a coherent sentence. "Yeah, well, she fooled all of us."

It was still hard for me to believe that Layne and Honor had fallen in love, even though you could see it when they were together. There had been so much animosity at first, but they said that love and hate were two sides of the same coin. I'd just never seen a couple that so embodied that in real life.

Layne's phone went off and she looked at the message and laughed.

"Who's that?" I asked, assuming it was Honor.

"Lark," she said. "She sends me funny stories about customers when she's bored."

"How's the job going?" I asked. Lark was taking a break from college and was desperate for independence, so Liam, Layne's brother had hooked her up with a job as a barista. Lark's work ethic was a little different from her sister's. When you saw the two of them together, they didn't even seem related, even though the family resemblance was there.

"It's good. She's doing her absolute best, but I think it's an adjustment for her. I would never tell Honor this, but when she took on all the responsibility for Lark, she deprived Lark of learning how to take care of herself and it's coming back to bite her in the ass."

Layne frowned. I could sense this was something she'd been holding onto.

"I know she thought she was doing the right thing, after

their monster of a mother did her best to screw both of them up, so I can't fault her for that."

Honor and Lark's mother sounded like a real piece of work from everything Layne, Lark, and Honor had told me. A cold and brutal woman who was determined to make her daughters the same way.

Fortunately, she had failed.

"She'll figure it out," I said. "Everyone does."

"You're right. I just can't help wanting to step in, but both Honor and Liam are telling me to stay out of it and I'm going to do that. I am keeping my opinions to myself." She crossed her arms as if to punctuate her statement.

When it came to staying out of other people's business (especially people she loved) and not trying to barge in and fix things, Layne was not an expert. It was one of the reasons we were such good friends. We each meddled in our own way. Hers involved a lot more cooking food, and mine involved a lot more planning behind the scenes and deep conversations.

"Don't say anything," Layne said, pointing at me.

I put my hands up. "I wasn't going to say anything."

Layne narrowed her eyes. "We've known each other long enough for me to know what you're going to say before you say it, Joy Catherine."

I cringed at her use of my first and middle name.

"That power goes both ways, Layne Alice," I threw back at her.

We pretended to glare at each other until we both burst out laughing.

"Okay, I should get back to work," I said, disposing of the rest of my salad.

"I probably should too," she said.

"At least you get to flirt with a beautiful woman on your breaks," I said. Honor was still working as Layne's boss,

Mark's, assistant, so they got to see each other all day while they were working most weeks.

"Hey, you never know who's going to walk into the bookshop," Layne said.

Maybe Ezra would walk in today. I hadn't heard from her since our little email exchange last night and I was trying not to read too much into it.

My phone rang and it was my mom. I ignored it and decided that before I talked to her, I needed to get some basic information from Ezra to make this whole thing believable. We had to keep our stories consistent so my family wouldn't sense that anything was up.

"Your mom again?" Layne said as she walked me back to the bookstore.

"Yup," I said. "If I don't call her back soon, she's going to show up at the bookstore and make a scene." My mom was not above publicly embarrassing any of her children. I guess that's what happened when you'd raised four daughters.

Layne gave me a sympathetic look. Her parents were involved in her life, but they weren't "make a scene" people. Unlike my mom. My dad, on the other hand, was the one who would stand in the corner while my mother was making a scene and quietly say "Sarah, that's enough" without actually intervening or making her stop.

I needed to get in touch with Ezra, so I sent her a quick email saying that we might need to meet again, or at least come up with a story of how we'd met, and I was going to need some personal details to flesh out the narrative for my family.

The bookstore was busy that afternoon, so I didn't get a chance to check my phone for a while. I was in the back organizing books for a signing the next night when Kendra came back and leaned in the doorway.

"Hey, there's someone out here for you. A very attractive someone." She wiggled her eyebrows.

My heart leapt and I knew that it had to be Ezra.

"Go on, you can finish this later," Kendra said. She really was a great boss.

I walked out to find Ezra running her finger along the spines of the books, her head tilted so she could read the titles and author names.

"Hey," I breathed, and she looked up at me.

"Hey, I figured I'd find you here," she said. "Do you have a few minutes?"

I nodded quickly. "Absolutely."

Since there weren't really any private places in the main part of the bookstore, I took Ezra back to the stockroom where I'd been working, avoiding Kendra's eyes as they followed both of us.

"The inner sanctum," Ezra said as I closed the door behind her.

"Not really. Just the stockroom," I said, gesturing around at the boxes and shelves of books and shipping materials we used for online or pickup orders.

"Your email seemed kind of urgent, so I came over," Ezra said.

"I appreciate that. My mom is blowing up my phone and I need to get back to her, so I thought we should come up with a story," I said, leaning against a table.

"A story?" Ezra asked, glancing around at the books.

"Yeah, I'm not going to tell my family that I paid someone to be my wedding date, so I need to have a plausible story to tell them about how we met, and so forth."

"Right. I had forgotten about that part." Her eyes swung around and met mine. "I'm sure you have an idea of what to say, so I'll just follow your script."

I nodded. "Okay. I figured we should stay close to the

truth. You came into the bookstore, I suggested a book, we started talking, so on and so forth." I really should have put more time into thinking about this, but I guess I'd thought it would be a more collaborative process.

"So on and so forth?" Ezra said. "Is that what the kids are calling it?"

I felt my face go completely red. "I wouldn't be telling my family about…that."

"But they're going to need to see some chemistry to know that it's not fake, don't you think?" Ezra said, suddenly stepping completely into my space.

I looked up into her eyes and suddenly didn't know how to swallow.

"That was the other thing we needed to talk about," I said, my voice sounding too loud in my own ears.

"You can't fake chemistry, Joy. You either have it or you don't."

She reached up and tucked some hair that had come out of the braid I'd done this morning behind my ear.

"Fortunately, I think we've got it. Don't you?" Ezra asked and it took me a moment to find the words to answer.

"I-I think so," I said, my voice stuttering.

Ezra smiled. "So now that we've gotten that out of the way, I think we should discuss boundaries. How far do you want to take this?"

That was a damn good question.

"Well," I said, trying not to fall completely into Ezra's eyes, "I think kissing should be on the table, don't you? My family would think it was strange if we didn't kiss."

"I think so. But we should probably practice, don't you think? First kisses can be awkward. It can take some time to figure out how you fit together."

I agreed, nodding and trying not to lick my lips. They felt dry.

"Then we're on the same page, Joy," Ezra said, and I got that little thrill every time she used my name. I'd heard my name thousands of times in my life, but never the way Ezra said it.

I fought back a hysterical giggle about the page comment, since we were surrounded by books.

Ezra leaned a fraction of an inch closer.

"How is now for a little practice?" she said.

"Okay," I blurted out way too eagerly. Ezra laughed softly as I moved closer to her. My eyes shuttered closed and then a sound made them fly open and spring away from Ezra as if I'd been shoved.

A knock at the door.

I stumbled toward it and opened it a crack. It was Kendra with an apologetic look on her face.

"I'm so sorry, but your mom is here."

This was my nightmare.

"Joy?" Kendra said, after a few seconds of me standing there in complete panic.

"Yeah, I'll be right out," I said, and she nodded. I closed the door and pressed my back up against it for support.

Now my hands were shaking for a different reason.

"Everything okay?" Ezra asked, opening the cover of one of the picture books on the table and then shutting it.

"My mom is here," I said. "My mom is here and you're here and oh my god, I can't believe this is happening."

I covered my face with my hands and wished I'd never even started this fake date business.

Ezra pulled my hands away from my face. "Hey," she said. "Don't worry about this. If you want me to escape out the back, I can do that. If you want me to come with you and stand by your side, I'll do that."

I stared at her, unable to comprehend what she was saying. "Why would you do that?"

She was still just a stranger I was paying money to be my date. We didn't know each other. I didn't even have her phone number, didn't know where she lived, didn't know what she did for work, didn't know anything about her family. We hadn't gotten to that part yet! I wasn't ready to introduce her to my mom.

"You seem really freaked out right now," Ezra said.

"I'm fine," I said, wiping my palms against my jeans. "I'm fine."

"I'll go," Ezra said.

That seemed a little dramatic. The way I was reacting, Ezra probably thought my mom was some kind of monster.

"No, no, it's okay. You don't have to run away. I'm just making a big deal out of nothing."

I took a few deep breaths as Ezra waited. I put a smile on my face.

"Okay, let's do this."

I opened the door and drew on all the confidence and that one semester I'd been in drama club to sell this to my mom.

"Joy-Joy, there you are," she said.

Just as I was about to open my mouth, Ezra slipped her hand into mine and squeezed my fingers. That simple gesture grounded me and my heart stopped racing like someone was chasing it.

"Hi, Mom. I'm sorry I haven't gotten back to you. I've been really busy," I said. "You didn't have to drive all the way here." Mom was partially retired, but still worked a few days a week as a receptionist at the local dentist office in Redfield. Guess this was her day off.

Mom looked at me and then Ezra and gave me a look. "I'm sure you have been. It's nice to meet you, Busy," Mom said.

"Nice to meet you too, Mrs. Greene. Joy's told me so many wonderful things."

I'd chosen well in my selection for a fake wedding date. Ezra's voice was filled with so much sincerity that I almost believed her.

"It's lovely to meet you, but I confess that my daughter has been avoiding my calls so I don't know much about you," Mom said, her eyes narrowing dangerously.

"I've just been really busy," I said, the panic starting to seep back in. Mom was going to know something was up. This had been a ridiculous plan. She was going to see right through me.

"That's my fault. I've been keeping her to myself," Ezra said, pulling me closer. I rested my back against her and she felt…solid.

Mom kept gazing at me, waiting for me to speak. I wasn't normally this quiet around her.

"So, um, was there something you needed?" I asked.

"Yes, I wanted to confirm that you did have a date and find out when we could meet this mysterious Ezra that no one seems to know anything about."

I cringed and hoped Ezra wasn't offended.

"I just moved here and Joy has been showing me around. I haven't lived in a town this small in a long time and it's nice to feel like I could become part of the community."

I almost swiveled my head to give her a look. Was she really laying it on thick, or was that true?

This was the problem with hiring a wedding date and not having her fill out an application at the beginning. My complete lack of planning was biting me in the ass.

"That's lovely," Mom said, and I finally found my voice.

"We were just talking that Ezra should come over for dinner," I said, waiting for her to flinch. That hadn't been included in my required list of wedding activities, but maybe she'd let me pay her a little bit extra for a family dinner.

Mom smiled. "Oh good. That was just what I was hoping you'd say. So, we'll see you on Sunday around seven?"

The words were said in a way that did not allow for any answer except "yes, we'll see you there."

"I'm free," Ezra said, squeezing my hand again.

"We'll see you there," I said, nodding.

"Wonderful. Your sisters will be so excited. Now give me a hug, I've got to get to the grocery store."

I had to let go of Ezra to hug Mom. "She's tall," Mom commented in my ear before she let me go. There was a twinkle in her eye, and I was thrown off guard.

"Ezra, are you okay with hugs?" Mom asked.

"Uh, sure," Ezra said, and hugged my mom. Well. That was unexpected. I wasn't sure if Mom said anything to Ezra, but when Ezra stepped back, there was a smile on her face.

"We'll talk more on Sunday. Be prepared for a lot of personal questions. We're not a family with good boundaries," Mom said, laughing.

"Mom!" I said. "You're going to freak her out."

Mom looked Ezra up and down, and I know she didn't miss the tattoos on Ezra's knuckles.

"She looks like a girl who doesn't scare easily," Mom said, patting my shoulder.

"I'm not, for the record," Ezra said, turning to look at me.

"Well, okay," I said, flummoxed by this whole interaction. "I should probably get back to work."

"Don't be too busy to call your mother back," Mom said, giving me one last kiss on the cheek before heading out of the bookstore.

I didn't exhale until the door closed.

"She isn't that bad," Ezra said. "Were you really that worried?"

"Believe me, she's only luring you with a false sense of security. One minute you're sitting down to cookies, and the next you're spilling your deepest, darkest secrets. She has her ways."

I always thought that my mother would have made a great detective, or even a lawyer. She was good at getting information out of people without them even realizing.

Ezra let out a deep breath. "I think I can handle her. Are you okay with all of this?"

She was asking about me?

"I mean, I'm not the one who's going to have to have dinner with a strange family. You didn't sign up for that. I'll understand if you want to change our agreement."

Ezra leaned on a shelf. "I'll throw in the family dinner for free. Call it a gesture of good faith. Does that work for you?"

"If you're okay with it, then I'm okay with it. But we definitely need to have a meeting now and get all our details right."

Ezra's phone went off and she pulled it out of her back pocket to read the message. She typed out a quick response and then her attention was back on me.

"Sounds like a plan. What are you doing on Friday night?"

My plan had been to hang out with Sydney and Layne, as I usually did. Honor was going away this weekend with Mark on a business trip, so Layne was solo and wanted us to be around. She wasn't very good at being alone, and I was more than happy to be backup for Honor.

"I was going to hang out with my friends, but I can cancel," I said. Or I could just meet with Ezra and go over to Layne's later. We usually hung out at her house since she loved cooking for us, and she had easy pool access.

"You shouldn't have to cancel on your friends. What about during the day?" Ezra said. For a fake wedding date, she sure was considerate.

"My lunch break is at twelve-thirty. Are you free then?" I asked. I still had no idea what she did all day, if anything. My mom hadn't been wrong about Ezra being mysterious.

"Should I meet you here?" Ezra asked. I nodded and she

leaned into me. The scent of some warm spice overwhelmed me. Cinnamon? Cloves? Something like that.

"We'll work on the kissing later. I didn't want you to think I'd forgotten."

She brushed her hand down my back and I melted into her, looking up into her eyes.

"Later," she said. It was both a goodbye and a promise.

"Joy?" Kendra's voice said, cutting through the bubble I'd been standing in with Ezra.

"Coming," I called back.

"Bye, Joy," Ezra said in a low voice and stepped away from me. I waited until she left before I sagged against a shelf to get myself back together.

Ezra completely undid me whenever she was near. I couldn't say that the feeling was entirely unpleasant. No, it was pretty much the opposite.

I closed my eyes and breathed again before going to see what Kendra needed.

∼

"LISTEN, if this leads to you getting laid, you should absolutely ditch me and Layne," Sydney said that night as I made dinner and she fed Clementine.

"I thought you were convinced she was a scammer five minutes ago?" I asked.

Sydney looked up from where she'd been petting Clementine as he ate his food.

She shrugged. "I changed my mind."

"I can't believe she's coming with me to family dinner. I'm sure she's going to completely bail afterwards, but at least I'll have a reason for not having a date, so it'll work out either way."

Ezra was tough, but sitting through an awkward, loud

dinner with a family you didn't know could make anyone run for the hills. Let's just say I was glad that I wasn't standing in her Converse.

"Oh, she'll be fine. Your family is not that scary," Syd said.

"Excuse me, do you not remember running away from Christmas dinner?" I asked.

Sydney glared. "It wasn't Christmas dinner, and I didn't run away. It was before Christmas and I got in my car and drove away. There's a difference."

I snorted. "You bailed. Just admit it. You bailed because my family is too much."

My family was too much for me a lot of the time.

Sydney hopped up to sit on the counter. "Okay fine, your family is a lot. But have you met my mother?"

That was true. If anyone could give my mom a run for her money, it was Syd's mom. If we got the two of them in the same space at the same time for too long, it might rip a hole in the universe from too-muchness.

"I still don't know anything about her, except she told my mom she just moved here," I said.

"Why don't you just stalk her on social media like a normal person?" Syd asked, grabbing a grape tomato and popping it into her mouth.

"I don't know," I said, avoiding the question.

"I bet I know why. You don't want to find out something you don't want to know. I know you, Joy. If there's something you don't want to see, you just put your head down and don't look at it."

I wanted to smack her with the spatula.

"I don't do that," I said, my voice sounding whiny in my ears.

"You absolutely do that, Joy, but it's okay. I love you anyway."

I blew out a breath and focused on stirring veggies in a pan that didn't really need to be stirred that much.

"Is it pick on Joy's flaws night?" I grumbled and Sydney put her arms around me.

"Don't be a grump. I shouldn't have said that. I'm sorry."

"It's okay," I said. "You didn't say anything I didn't already know. I just wish I could forget this whole wedding thing and have it be over."

"Yes, but then you wouldn't get to see Ezra in a suit. I've heard she's pretty hot," Syd said and then smacked my butt. "Go get it, Joy."

"Sydney. This is a business arrangement. It's not like that," I said, but I could feel the blush creeping across my cheeks.

Sydney rolled her eyes. "Oh yeah, like you're not completely attracted to her."

"Being attracted to her has nothing to do with it," I said, staring directly into the pan.

"You are so full of shit. The reason you even propositioned her was that she was hot and you were thinking with your downstairs instead of your brain. Which, good for you. More people should do that. Some of my best nights were made when I turned my brain off and listened to her," Sydney said, pointing to her lower half.

"Gross, Syd. I don't want to think about that, thank you very much."

The vegetables were going to burn to a crisp if I cooked them any more, so I turned the stove off and plated them up with some chicken I'd cooked in another pan. Everything got dumped on a bed of rice. Tonight had been a "lazy meal" night.

Sydney added some parmesan cheese and a few shots of hot sauce. I just added a little bit of cheese and skipped the sauce.

"You could hook up with her, you know," Sydney said.

"Are we still talking about this? I'm not you, Sydney," I said, blowing on a piece of chicken.

"Yeah, but you should let your hair down. Just once. Just promise me you'll consider it."

Oh I'd considered it. I'd been woken up in the middle of the night aching from how much I'd considered it.

But I wasn't Sydney. I wasn't the kind of person who could just have a one-night stand and go on my merry way. No matter how much I'd tried before, my feelings got involved and then everything was a giant mess.

No, I wasn't "hit and quit it" like Sydney. I was a more "complete and utter love at first sight" kind of woman, and I wished I wasn't that way. It would be so nice to just have a good, sweaty time with someone and then leave without thinking of them ever again. I had needs just like everyone else and there was only so much my hands and a vibrator could do. A vibrator couldn't hold you, skin-to-skin as you fell asleep. A vibrator didn't make you feel safer than you'd ever been. A vibrator didn't make jokes during coitus that made you laugh and realize sex didn't have to be so serious.

Now, if someone could make a vibrator that could do all those things, I'd be first in line to order it, but until then, I was on my own and Ezra was off-limits. Couldn't go mixing business with pleasure like that.

I still didn't know how I was going to go about kissing her and making it believable, but also keeping myself neutral, but I was going to suck it up and be an adult and do it. Like a little challenge for myself. Weren't all of those personal development books touting the power of being uncomfortable? Sure, those books were mostly bullshit, but just maybe I could pull this off.

ANOTHER EMAIL from Ezra came through late that night. I'd just written a little bit in my gratitude journal and set it aside.

Do you have any food allergies?
-Ezra

Why was she asking me about food allergies? It seemed completely out of the blue.

No, I don't have any food allergies. Can I ask what prompted that question?

The more I learned about Ezra, the more interested and perplexed I became.

I'm bringing you lunch, but I didn't want to poison you. Do you have any food preferences?

She was bringing me lunch? That was an awfully nice thing for a fake wedding date to do.

You don't have to bring me lunch. I should probably be bringing you lunch, I replied.

Let me bring you lunch, Joy. You're not very good at accepting people doing things for you, are you?

Ezra was beginning to sound like Sydney.

The rainbow veggie and hummus wrap from the café is my favorite.

There. No one could accuse me of not accepting lunch when I told her what my favorite thing was.

You got it. I'll be there tomorrow.

Chapter Five

"You seem shiny this morning," Sydney commented as I hummed to myself and stirred scrambled eggs in a pan.

"Do I?" I asked.

"Could it have anything to do with a certain person who's agreed to be your fake wedding date?" Sydney said, raising one dark eyebrow.

"I will neither confirm nor deny," I said.

"Ha, so that means yes," Sydney said, cackling.

"I have no idea what you're talking about," I said, dumping eggs on her plate. Sydney added her requisite hot sauce as I cringed.

"I don't know how you can eat that in the morning."

"That's because you have no taste," Sydney said, shoveling eggs into her mouth and closing her eyes in bliss. "Perfect."

I ate my eggs plain and then Sydney badgered me as we walked downstairs and parted ways to our respective jobs.

"You're all giddy today," Kendra said as soon as I walked in. Guess I wasn't so good at hiding my excitement. Hopefully I could tone it down before Ezra showed up.

I just shrugged and Kendra waited.

"Ezra is bringing me lunch and we're discussing our plan," I said. Kendra knew all about the wedding date situation, and she'd promised to swear Theo to secrecy. I wasn't worried they'd blow my cover. Only a handful of people knew and I trusted them not to blab. Plus, it was nice to have a few people to talk with about how bonkers the situation was.

"I can't believe you're doing this. It's so not you," Kendra said as we readied the shop.

"I know. I think that's one of the reasons I'm doing it," I said.

"That's kind of how things were with Theo. Going after her was really out of character for me, but I'm damn glad that I did," Kendra said. "Sometimes you need to take a risk, and you can't explain why."

"Well, your risk turned out different than mine will. I'm just in need of a wedding date, nothing else," I said.

Kendra gave me a look. "That's what you think, but life has a way of giving you what you need even when you make other plans."

"She's off-limits," I said, but Kendra just shook her head and went to unlock the door and turn the sign to say 'Open.'

~

THE CLOSER IT got to my lunch break, the more anxious I got. I knew I was making a bigger deal out of this than it was, but I was still waiting for Ezra to call everything off and tell me that she'd changed her mind. Even with the incentive of a thousand dollars, I was asking a lot.

"I'm heading out," I told Kendra at one minute before twelve-thirty and she told me to have a good lunch.

Ezra wasn't in the front of the store, but I found her in the back, where there was a picnic table that we shared with some of the other businesses and a little smoking and vaping area for anyone who needed it.

She'd been leaning against the wall of the bookstore and looked up when I shut the door.

"Lunch is here," she said, holding up a bag. "Was there somewhere you wanted to sit?"

The picnic table was never cleaned and covered in bird crap from seagulls eating the crumbs left over from old sandwiches.

"Not here," I said, gesturing at the table. There weren't a whole lot of outdoor seating areas that weren't attached to the shops, so I said that we could go up to my apartment. On days when I had bad customers, sometimes I'd run upstairs and give myself a break, and sometimes I'd go up and pull something out of the fridge for lunch if I hadn't had a moment to pack anything. It was handy living so near to where you worked.

Ezra followed me upstairs and I told her to stand back so I didn't let Clementine out. He could be an escape artist and had been found wandering around outside on the sidewalk more than once.

Clementine immediately screamed at me for food, even though he had an automatic feeder during the day.

"Sir, you are fine," I told him.

"Who is this distinguished gentleman?" Ezra asked, crouching down to hold her hand out to Clementine, who eyed her suspiciously before coming over to sniff her fingers.

"That's Clementine and don't believe a word he says," I said as Clementine bumped his head against Ezra's knee and she stroked the top of his head.

"Oh, are you a little liar?" Ezra said in a soft voice.

"He is," I said, getting some plates out of the cupboards. "Did you want to sit at the counter or on the couch?"

"I'm a creature of comfort," Ezra said, looking up at me, still petting a loudly purring Clementine. He'd decided Ezra was a friend who might feed him, so now she was his new favorite.

"Couch it is," I said, and Ezra followed me into the living room. She pulled out the wraps from the bag as well as two cans of soda.

"I didn't know what you'd like, so you can pick," she said.

"I'd rather die than drink that," I said, pointing to one of the cans before taking the other.

"Okay, Joy's soda preferences are noted," Ezra said with a laugh.

"Thanks for bringing me food," I said as I pulled my wrap out. Ezra had gotten the same thing.

"Seemed like the least I could do," she said, turning her head and taking a bite.

We both ate in relative silence, punctuated only by Clementine making noise and the ticking of the clock.

"Who's the artist?" Ezra asked, pointing at several watercolors that hung on the wall.

"Sydney's mom. She owns the pottery shop downstairs, and Syd manages it. She didn't inherit any of the artistic genes."

"Ouch," Ezra said. "That's got to be rough."

"Yeah, it's a tough subject for her, so we try not to bring it up."

Ezra asked me more about how long I'd lived with Sydney, when I'd started working at the bookstore, if I liked it.

"I moved here six years ago and was sort of bouncing around and doing random jobs for a while, but when I heard about Kendra opening the bookstore, I knew I really wanted to work there. I have retail experience and I love books so it seemed like the perfect match. That she's such a good boss is a bonus. I love my job."

"I can tell," Ezra said. "Your face lights up when you talk about it."

"Oh," I said. "I'm not good at hiding any of my emotions.

No one in my family is. We're also not shy about sharing them out loud either."

"How many sisters do you have again?"

This was information she was definitely going to need to know.

"Three. And then Mom and Dad and that makes six of us. Anna is the one getting married to Robert. He's very sweet and very boring. Don't tell her I said that."

Ezra pressed her lips together to hide a smile. "I wouldn't dream of it."

"The wedding is going to be very basic, I'm going to warn you. My sister doesn't have a ton of imagination, so she's just copying a lot of what my two older sisters have done, and what her friends have done."

"So all your sisters are married?"

I nodded since my mouth was full. "Yup, and my mother is very concerned about my prospects."

Ezra let out a snort. "Is she now?"

"Yes," I said. "So don't be surprised if she badgers you about your intentions. She doesn't want me going out with anyone who isn't serious about commitment."

For the first time, Ezra frowned as she set down her wrap and wiped her hands on a napkin.

"How much do you want me to lie to your family?" she asked.

"As much as you need to. I figure we say what we need to say to get through the wedding and then a few days later I can tell them we had a fight and we're not together anymore," I said. Ezra popped the top of the awful soda.

"We could have a public breakup. Make it more believable," Ezra said.

"No way. I'm not that good of an actress. I'm also not the 'make a scene' kind of person. Unlike my mother and a couple of my sisters." They liked to compete for who could embarrass me most in public. So far they were all tied.

"No public breakup. So why are we breaking up? That has to be realistic," she said.

"I figured I could tell them that you were cheating on me," I said, and waited for Ezra's reaction.

"Oh, I see how it is, blame everything on me. I think I should get a bonus for that," she said.

"Kidding! I wouldn't do that," I said. "But if you'd gone for it, I might have. I figured I could just say that we were on different paths and didn't see eye-to-eye on our future."

Ezra thought about that. "You could tell them that I decided I'm not ready for commitment. That wouldn't be a lie."

I turned on the couch so I could see her better.

"We've been talking a whole lot about me, but what about you? If you're going to be my wedding date, I should know at least a few facts, don't you think?"

Ezra leaned back on the couch and met my gaze, resting her arm on the back of the couch.

"What do you want to know?"

"How old are you?" I asked. Not the best first question, but I had to start somewhere.

"Twenty-seven. You?"

"Twenty-six. Where are you from?"

"Originally? Western Massachusetts, but I've lived all over the US." That tracked with what she'd told my mom about settling down in a small town.

"What brought you to Arrowbridge?" There wasn't a whole lot here to lure someone like Ezra. It wasn't as if there were tons of job opportunities or a thriving nightlife. Everything pretty much closed down before nine at night. Things were a little lively during the summer season, but for the most part the best word to describe Arrowbridge was "quaint."

"I had never lived in Maine before and I searched a list of small towns. There was just something about it, so I booked a week vacation and moved here the week after."

"Seriously?" I asked.

Ezra nodded. "Seriously."

"Wow," I said. I couldn't even imagine doing something like that. Just picking a random town and moving there? I'd always moved where work took me.

"So far it's been great," she said. "I'll let you know how the winter goes. I'm not so sure about that."

"But you were born in New England, so you should be used to winters by now," I said. Ezra shuddered.

"I will never get used to the cold and the snow and being stuck inside the house because I don't feel like shoveling."

"I'll give you the name of the guy who shovels the sidewalks. He'll come over and take care of you."

"Thanks. I'd appreciate that," Ezra said. She went quiet and even though she was sitting on the couch with me, I could feel her pulling away.

Ezra didn't like to talk about herself. That was fine. I couldn't seem to shut up, but I did need more.

"So, since you're going to be meeting my family, what about yours?" I said.

"Mmm, we're not close. Let's leave it at that?" she said.

"That's fair enough. I'll let my family know so they won't pry. Too much." They were definitely going to bother her a little bit about it.

"It's fine," Ezra said, and her hand clenched on the couch cushion. "So, why don't you give me a rundown on your family so I can be prepared for Sunday."

The abrupt change back to me didn't surprise me, but I did note it.

"Okay, so Faith is the oldest..." I started.

BY THE TIME I gave Ezra a primer on my sisters, my lunch break was almost over and I needed to get back to work.

"What are you doing for the rest of the day?" I asked as Ezra helped me take the plates and the leftovers to the kitchen.

"This and that," she said, handing me a plate. I set it in the dishwasher and then rinsed off my hands.

"My family is going to ask you a ton of invasive questions. Are you ready for that?"

Ezra leaned down to pet Clementine again. Just behind his ears, which he loved.

"I think I can handle it. I'm a big girl, Joy."

She stood up and suddenly she was in my space again, and I'd lost the ability to form a coherent thought. We had just been eating wraps on the couch and now I could hear my heart pounding in my ears.

"You know, we didn't get to the kiss practicing," she said, walking me backwards until I was up against the counter.

"I have to get back to work," I said, and then wanted to kick myself. If anyone would understand me being late for work because I was busy kissing someone, it was Kendra. She'd been late a few times and blamed everything on Theo. Kendra really was a great boss.

"Mmm, then we should meet up again later. What about Sunday morning?"

Wait, what day was today? I didn't even know.

"Sure," I agreed, because I couldn't think of anything I could possibly be doing on Sunday that would prevent me from being with Ezra and getting a chance to practice kissing with her.

"Okay," she said, leaning down as if she was going to kiss me, but swerving away from my mouth at the last second.

"I'll see you on Sunday," she said in my ear, and I couldn't move. I couldn't speak. I couldn't even breathe.

Ezra pulled back and winked. "Have a good rest of your day, Joy."

She walked through the door, making sure she didn't let Clementine out. He yowled after her as I gripped the counter until my fingers hurt.

"Holy shit," I said.

My phone went off, startling me. Kendra was just checking in to see when I'd be back.

Coming right now I sent to her as I said goodbye to Clementine and locked the front door.

~

"OKAY, SO TELL ME EVERYTHING," Layne said as she handed me a glass of wine. Sydney and I were sitting on the couch in her house and she'd pulled out a charcuterie board that she'd ordered from some fancy company Honor had turned her on to.

My two best friends stared at me with expectant eyes.

"I mean, she still hasn't told me much. I'm kind of curious to see if she can withstand my mom's techniques."

"I almost wish I could be there to see it. You'll have sneak off and give us updates," Layne said. "But back to this Ezra. I think I saw her in the library once. From what you told me about her, she's kind of hard to miss."

Despite the sheer number of queer people in Arrowbridge, they were more rural queers and Ezra had the scent of having been everywhere about her. Plus, the tattoos. They weren't that unusual, but you were much more likely to see an anchor or a pinup girl than wildflowers.

Ezra did have the flannel uniform down, but her flannel wasn't as worn as what regular Arrowbridge residents sported.

"I did some eavesdropping in the shop, and everyone is buzzing that someone young and new and apparently single has moved in," Sydney said. "If she comes into the shop, Mom even has a plate set aside to give to her as a welcome present."

"That's so sweet," Layne said. "It's making me want to bake her a basket of muffins or something."

"What about brownies?" I asked. Layne had a thing for brownies.

Layne grinned. "Brownies are just for Honor now."

The timer on the oven went off and she got up to pull out the chicken pot pie she'd made for us. Instead of a crust, it was topped with homemade biscuits and my mouth was watering just thinking about digging into a huge bowl of it.

"Well, I'm intrigued by her," Sydney said. "She's not my type, but I do love a good mystery."

Whenever we got a new cozy mystery book in at the bookstore, I always put aside a copy for Syd. She devoured them in an afternoon and I was jealous of her reading speed.

Layne brought over our plates and put on a movie, but we weren't really watching it. She and Sydney were trading theories about Ezra.

"My vote is witness protection. That explains everything. This is the perfect place to get completely lost in," Sydney said.

"Getting lost in Arrowbridge? With all the gossips running around?" Layne said, lifting one eyebrow. "Not very likely."

"The gossips haven't figured out who Ezra is yet, so they can't be that good," Sydney fired back.

"I still think she's running from a haunted past. A broken heart, maybe," Layne said. Of course she would say that. It made a lot more sense than witness protection. Sydney had to be dramatic.

"I think you've both read too many books," I said, and they gave me looks.

"What? I have both feet firmly rooted in reality," I said.

Both Layne and Sydney shared a look. "Out of the three of us, you are literally the most romantic, what are you talking about?" Layne said.

"You literally fart tiny hearts," Sydney said.

"Gross. And untrue," I said. "Okay, so I may be a little starry-eyed when it comes to love and romance, but that's different than thinking Ezra is in the witness protection program."

Sydney snorted. "That's what you think. I'd much sooner believe in witness protection than the kind of love you're talking about."

I shook my head. "You're too cynical, Syd."

"And I think you're not cynical enough."

"And I'm just the right amount of cynical," Layne announced. "Cheers to that." We each raised our glasses and clinked them together.

～

SYDNEY and I crashed on the pull-out couch, which was even nicer than my bed at home. Layne technically lived in the guest house of her employer, and he was rich as hell, so his guest house was extremely nice. Sure, it wasn't exactly her taste, but she had a gigantic King-sized bed that could fit a whole family plus dogs.

The only bed I could fit into my room in my apartment was a full, and I hated it every day.

"You thinking about Ezra?" Sydney teased as we lay in bed reading together. She had a used cozy mystery with a worn spine and I had my e-reader with an advanced copy of a new sapphic fantasy series that I was extremely excited about. One of the best perks of being a bookseller was getting to read all the books, when I had the time.

"No, I was reading," I said, making sure I'd flagged my place before turning to look at her.

"I still think you should go for it."

I hadn't told Syd or Layne about the whole kissing practice thing. I knew that would give them ammunition to make all kinds of assumptions and tease me until the end of time, so I kept my mouth shut. They didn't need to know mine and Ezra's business.

"I'm not talking about this anymore," I said, going back to my book.

"Oh, we are definitely still talking about this," Sydney said, laughing.

"I'm ignoring you now," I said, my voice loud.

"Stop fighting," Layne called from the bedroom. She'd left the door open a little bit and every now and then she'd yell a random comment at us and we'd have a conversation through the door. She really sucked at being alone.

"Yes, Miss Layne," Sydney called back in a mocking voice.

"Don't start with me, Sydney," Layne said. "I'll sic my girlfriend on you and she'll stab you with a stiletto."

"Ohhh, be careful," I told Sydney.

"I could take her," Sydney said.

"That's what she wants you to think," Layne called. "Lure you into a false sense of security."

"I still think I could take her," Sydney said.

I kept my mouth shut because my money was on Honor. She was craftier than Sydney, and better at hiding her emotions. Honor had relaxed a lot since we'd gotten to know her, but there was still a veil of distance between her and the world. Except when she looked at Layne.

"Of course you could," I said, patting her arm.

Sydney narrowed her eyes and made a huffing noise and went back to reading her book.

THE TEMPERATURES WERE in the upper seventies the next day, unusual for this time of year, but perfect for us since we had a whole pool to ourselves.

Riley and Zoey were with their mother for the weekend, so Layne didn't have her attention divided, and we could sneak into the main house for drink mixes and extra snacks.

"Which one of you is going to get rich so we can live like this all the time?" Layne asked as she handed out rum punches to each of us. I had to admit, being Layne's friend, I was pretty spoiled.

"Won't be me," Sydney said. "Unless someone famous comes into the shop and makes us go viral. I keep telling Mom we should be sending boxes to influencers, but then I have to explain what an influencer is and then we end up fighting about social media and I give up."

"Oh, so it's my responsibility? How many millionaire book-sellers do you know?" I asked.

"There's that one guy who started that online store," Layne pointed out.

"Yeah, but fuck him," Sydney said.

"I'd rather not," I said, cringing.

"Gross!" Layne said, shaking her head. "Let's not ruin the day with talk of billionaires. None of us needs that much. But if one of us could, say, find a famous painting at a yard sale, or maybe invest in something that pays off?"

"So, win the lottery, is what you're saying," Sydney said. "I don't have good luck."

"I'll be on the lookout for old books that might be worth a lot of money," I said. Kendra did a small business of used and rare books in a corner of the shop. Every now and then we would hit up garage and estate sales and add to the collection.

Sometimes the library would give us some overflow books that they didn't have room for in their little used bookshop.

"Yes, see if you can find, like, a really old copy of Pride and Prejudice," Sydney said.

"Jax has one," Layne said. Jax and her wife, Sasha, lived just one town over in Hartford, and Jax taught school, but her father was the famous author Jack Hill. She had an incredible library that I'd gotten to see and I was eaten up with jealousy about.

"Of course she does," Sydney said, rolling her eyes and dipping another chip in the dip that Layne had whipped up. "You should just get really good at forgery. I've seen a couple of documentaries." This was directed at me.

"I'm not doing anything illegal," I said. "Absolutely not."

"Yeah, let's not do any scams," Layne said. "If only I'd let Honor marry Mark. Then she could have gotten alimony."

We all laughed. Honor had gone for Mark, originally, and mostly for his money. Then she'd fallen for Layne and abandoned that plan, and Mark and his ex-wife had reconciled, which really was the best situation for all involved.

"Maybe Ezra is rich," Layne said. "Maybe she inherited a fortune and she's looking for someone to share it with."

I stared at her from behind my sunglasses. "Layne. If she was rich, then why did she suggest that I pay her as the condition of her being my wedding date?"

Layne thought about that for a second. "Because she had to keep up appearances. It's all a ruse."

That didn't seem very likely at all, but if Layne wanted to write that little fanfiction, I wasn't going to rain on her parade.

"I still think she's in witness protection. That's my story and I'm sticking to it," Sydney said, finishing her drink.

"I think both of you are wrong," I said.

"Then it's your job to find out," Sydney said, pointing at me.

WE DIDN'T SPEND the whole day talking about Ezra theories, thankfully. We hit up the farmers' market and had lunch as we walked around and then soaked in the pool for a little while.

"I can't wait until it's cold enough for the hot tub," Layne said as we leaned against the edge of the pool.

"Soon," Sydney said. "I can't wait for it to snow."

Layne and I both made faces.

"I don't know how you can enjoy the snow. It makes everything annoying," Layne said.

"Oh stop, Mark shovels your car out for you every time," Sydney said, waving her off.

"It's still annoying," Layne said, and I agreed. I hated waking up and looking outside knowing that I was going to have to hack a half-inch of ice off my car before I could get to the grocery store. New England winters could be brutal and even though I'd lived my whole life with them, that didn't make it any easier.

"I can't wait," Sydney said with a sigh. For someone who was very jaded about just about everything, she really held onto her childlike wonder when it came to winter. It was adorable.

Layne's phone went off and she hopped out of the pool to go check it.

"Stop sexting Honor," Sydney called out.

"We weren't sexting," Layne said, but her cheeks were red and she wouldn't make eye contact with me or Syd.

"I'll be…right back," she said cryptically, and vanished into the main house.

"Good for her," Sydney said.

"You sexting anyone these days?" I asked.

Sydney shook her head and then leaned back and looked

up at the sky. "No. I'm on a little bit of a hiatus. A sexual pause, if you will."

"You, taking a break?" This was the first I was hearing of it. Sydney loved hooking up. "Any reason for this break?"

Syd let out a sigh. "Just seemed like a good idea." That was pretty vague, but I could tell that even if I pushed, she wasn't going to give me more than that. When you pushed Syd for more than she wanted to give, she could get mean and I didn't feel like fighting with her right now. It was best to just let her be.

"Well, I hope that you're enjoying your sexual hiatus."

Syd frowned. "I'm not, really."

"So then why are you doing it?"

Layne came out again with her cheeks flushed and rejoined us in the pool.

"How's Honor?" Sydney asked.

"Fine," Layne said. "She was taking a break at the hotel and wanted to check in."

"And by check in, you mean she wanted to send you a picture of her boobs," Sydney said. I choked on my drink.

"No," Layne said, but I didn't believe her.

"Oh, come on, it's not a big deal," Sydney said. "Boobs for everyone!"

Layne shook her head, but she was smiling. "I guess we have to drink to that."

We toasted to boobs and I had to stop myself from wondering what exactly Ezra's boobs looked like.

Chapter Six

I HAD EMAILED BACK and forth with Ezra about Sunday morning, but she hadn't given me a definite time when she was coming over, so I woke up extremely early, just in case.

Sydney's door was open so Clementine could come and go, but I shut him in as he snuggled with Syd and hoped that he wouldn't make too much of a racket.

Ezra also hadn't told me where we were going to be practicing kissing. I couldn't really do it in my apartment with Sydney barging in. Sometimes she forgot to knock and then I'd never hear the end of it. Hopefully she had some ideas. Or maybe she'd take me to her place. I was really hoping she'd take me to her place since I was dying to see it.

At nine there was a knock at the door and I opened it to find Ezra holding a bakery bag and a tray with two iced coffees.

"Good morning," she said.

"Good morning," I said, breathing as if I'd just run up a flight of stairs. She wore a black tank and an open flannel shirt, looking like the lesbian lumberjack of my dreams.

I let her in and she set the bag and the coffees on the

counter. "No welcome committee?" she asked, and it took me a second to realize she meant Clementine.

"He's in the room with Sydney," I said in a low voice. "She's still asleep. Syd isn't a morning person, so she makes up for it on the weekends and sleeps in."

Ezra's eyes flicked to Syd's door.

"I was hoping you had somewhere more private in mind," I said, messing with the hem of my shirt.

"My car?" Ezra suggested.

"Not very private," I said. "Especially if it's parked in one of the lots around here." No doubt someone who knew my parents would see me kissing Ezra in a car and spread it all around town. Not that kissing in a car was illegal, but I knew I'd get a lecture from my mom about appropriate public behavior.

"I'm sure there's some place that people park their cars for this kind of thing? I assumed all small towns had a make-out spot," Ezra said, and the temperature of my blood rose a few degrees.

"There is," I said. "I've never been there, though."

Ezra picked up one of the coffees and sipped it through the straw. "Wanna go?"

I bit back a nervous giggle. "Uh, sure?"

Ezra grabbed the bag with her other hand. "Then what are we waiting for?"

Ezra followed me down to my car as I chatted and tried not to babble too much. Something about this was feeling very much like a date and I didn't want my brain to get the wires crossed.

This was just a task that we had to complete. Like the different events of the wedding: bridal shower, rehearsal dinner, wedding.

This was just another step we'd added.

I cringed at my car being a mess and hoped Ezra wasn't going to judge me too harshly.

"Sorry," I said as I unlocked her door.

Ezra just got in and pushed the seat back. "You should see my car when I'm traveling. This is nothing."

She put both our coffees in the cupholders and I took the first sip of mine, trying not to stress out about having coffee breath. Before she'd showed up, I'd brushed and flossed and swished mouthwash within an inch of my life. Like I was a tween before my first boy/girl party where someone would suggest we play Spin the Bottle.

I pulled onto Main Street and headed in the direction of the parking lot of one of the local nature trails. Arrowbridge had several, but this one was a little bit more hidden, and locals didn't generally share its location. Consequently, it had become popular with local teens looking to get into shenanigans without their parents' knowledge.

I felt like a jittery teen on my first date as I took a series of turns, driving onto more and more rural roads.

"Are you sure we aren't going to encounter any serial killers with chainsaws?" Ezra asked, looking out the window. It was the first time I'd ever seen her exhibit any kind of apprehension.

"Serial killers, no. Hunters wearing blaze orange looking for deer? Yes," I said. You had to be careful in Arrowbridge in the fall, especially if you had a pet.

"Seems just as dangerous," Ezra said, muttering under her breath.

"Your 'from away' side is showing," I said, amused by this turn of events. Anyone who wasn't born and raised in Maine was "from away" and that was that.

"So you're telling me the flannel hasn't fooled you that I'm a local?" she said, looking down at her shirt.

"It's too clean," I said. "And there aren't any holes."

"Hmm," Ezra said, still studying her shirt. "Well maybe you can give me lessons on how to fit in."

"You gonna charge me for them?" I asked as I went over a bump as I turned into the lot. The place was neglected and full of potholes and littered with the remnants of teens. Piles of bottles and other party detritus.

"Here we are," I said. Somehow, we were the only car in the lot. Not surprising, given it was Sunday morning.

"It's almost exactly as I pictured it," Ezra said. Along with several tires and a makeshift fire pit, the place is pretty much a dump.

"Not very romantic if you're over the age of seventeen," I said.

Ezra turned to look at me. "Who said it needs to be romantic? We just need private."

Right. This wasn't a date. This was a business meeting. Mouth-to-mouth business meeting.

"Sorry, I'm not really sure how to do this," I said, glancing over at her. The silence in my car felt heavy, like a blanket.

"You have kissed someone before, I assume," Ezra said.

"A few times," I said, wishing I'd used a lip mask last night. I'd forgotten.

"Then it's no big deal. I think people make far too much out of kissing, don't you?"

I wasn't so sure about that, but I nodded anyway.

"We're only doing this so we don't make a mistake in front of your family later," Ezra said.

"I'm not scared," I said. It felt like she was trying to coax me into this. She was right; a kiss wasn't a big deal. People kissed all the time, for all kinds of reasons.

"Then let's get started," Ezra said, her tone switching to very businesslike.

I leaned toward her and she stopped when she was just a few inches from my face.

"No tongue, agreed?" she asked, and it took me a second to process that she expected an answer.

"No tongue," I agreed. This just had to be a believable kiss. I wasn't the kind of person who made out with her date in front of her family anyway.

"Ready?" Ezra asked and I was shaking with the anticipation. If she didn't kiss me soon, I might combust from the stress.

I inhaled once before Ezra angled her head so our noses wouldn't bump and pressed her lips to mine. Once. Gently as a whisper.

She pulled back.

"There. How was that?" I couldn't tell her how it was. The kiss had been over before it even began.

"Fine," I said, lying.

Ezra studied my face. "Let's try again, shall we?"

"Yeah," I said.

This time, Ezra touched the side of my face with one hand. Her fingers were warm.

My lips trembled just a hint before she leaned in again. Ezra's mouth was firmer this time, and the contact lasted longer, but it was still over too soon. It was like getting handed an ice-cream cone and then having someone snatch it out of your hand just as if you were about to take a lick.

"Verdict?" Ezra asked. I didn't know why she was asking. Instead of answering her, I just grabbed the front of her shirt and pulled her toward me. Our noses bumped, but that didn't stop me.

Ezra let out a little startled gasp as my lips met hers and I slanted my mouth over hers to deepen the kiss. No tongue, but I was giving her everything else.

Ezra inhaled sharply through her nose and then it was like she lost all resistance. She practically crawled over the console toward me and the hand that had been on my face gripped the back of my neck, pulling me toward her. I'd completely lost control of the kiss and I was happy to let it happen.

Even after Ezra's tongue slipped into my mouth, I couldn't recall the rules we'd made. There had been rules, right?

She made a growling sound in the back of her throat as if she was going to devour me and I decided that if there had been rules, fuck it. Fuck anything that had gotten in the way of this kiss.

I wanted to get closer to her, but my car was in the way and at last the console digging into me couldn't be ignored. I'd done my best to crawl into Ezra's lap and failed.

"I'm sorry," I gasped as I broke the kiss. The smell of spilled coffee wafted up from the cupholders. In my quest to get closer to Ezra, I'd spilled both our drinks all over my car.

"Shit," I said. Ezra licked her lips and then let go of me. I still had my hand in her shirt and I made my fingers release it.

"Sorry," I said again. The coffee was going to be a mess to clean up, but I didn't care. Not even if my car smelled like rotting coffee for the next year. Worth it.

"It's okay," Ezra said, her voice unsteady. Her hair was up, but she pulled out the elastic, ran her hands through the strands, and then put it back up again. Her undercut was crisp, and I longed to run my fingers along the blunt edges of the hair on the back of her neck. I'd like to follow my fingers with my lips and tongue…

"I'm sorry too," Ezra said, looking a little more composed as I leaned down and picked up the now-empty cups.

"For what?" I asked.

"We agreed no tongue."

"We did," I said, pulling a bag from the back to toss the cups in. I could just chuck them out of the car to hang out with the rest of the trash, but I couldn't morally do that.

"Sorry about your coffee," I said.

Ezra waved that off. "It's fine. I can get more later."

She was silent as I cleaned up the rest of the coffee mess and tried to wipe down my car with some flimsy napkins. Guess it was time to take it to get detailed.

"Should we, um, should we go somewhere else?" Ezra said, her voice unsure. She sounded as rattled as I felt.

That kiss between us wasn't just a kiss. No, that was a promise and a threat. Wars had been waged upon kisses like that. People had crossed oceans for kisses like that. If my car hadn't interfered, I'd still be kissing Ezra. I couldn't see the point in spending my time doing anything else.

"Joy?" Ezra using my name made me snap back into the present moment.

"Oh, yeah, sure," I said, turning my car on and backing out of the lot. I had no idea where the fuck I was going, but my brain knew how to get back to downtown Arrowbridge.

Just as I was pulling into my usual parking spot, I got a text message from Sydney that she was heading out to do some errands so I had the apartment to myself for a few hours. I still hadn't eaten and I was starving, so I suggested that Ezra and I go upstairs and I could make her some coffee to replace what had spilled in my car.

"Sounds good," she said and followed me up the stairs and waited while I fumbled with my keys.

Clementine almost shot through the gap in the door, but I managed to push him back with my foot.

"No you don't, sir," I said as he yelled in protest as I foiled his escape plans.

"Has Sydney ever tried to put a harness on him and take him outside?" Ezra asked as I washed the rest of the coffee off my hands and dumped the trash from my car.

"Yes, and it was a disaster. He really believes he wants to be outside, but you take him out there and then he freaks out and wants nothing more than to hide under the bed again."

Sydney had tried so hard to get him to be the kind of cat

you could walk around on a leash and take on trips, but that just wasn't Clementine. He was a homebody cat.

"Poor Clementine," Ezra said and then turned her attention to me. Her eyes flicked down to my lips and then back up to meet my eyes.

I hoped she was thinking about the kiss. I sure was.

"Coffee," I said, remembering. "Making coffee."

"Sorry the burritos are probably cold," she said, pulling two wrapped packages out of the bag.

"That's okay. I can zap them for a few seconds," I said, adding water to the coffeemaker and then pointed to the basket of pods. "Grab whichever one you want."

Ezra picked through the pods and handed one to me, and I tried not to startle too much as our hands touched. I swore I could still feel the way she'd dug her fingers into the back of my neck as we kissed. If I looked in the mirror, would there still be marks? Part of me hoped so.

Ezra and I moved around each other in the tiny space, and I didn't want it to be awkward, but it was while we got everything set up. This time, Ezra put her coffee cup in front of one of the stools. Guess we weren't eating on the couch this time.

I joined her in the other chair, and Clementine hopped up to secure his seat at the third chair. He sniffed at our food and drinks and then curled up and shut his eyes with a sigh.

"Thanks for breakfast," I said, to break some of the silence. "Although I guess it's brunch now."

"You're welcome. So, what will your family be serving for dinner?" Oh. We were talking about that instead of talking about that kiss.

"Nothing too fancy. Mom usually just does a roast chicken with some carrots and potatoes or a roast or something. There will be biscuits and salad."

Ezra sipped her coffee and set it down before regarding her burrito. "Should I bring something?"

I shook my head. "No need. Mom gets mad if you bring things. She's weird that way. It's like insulting her ability to feed her children or something."

Ezra chewed and I bit into my own burrito. It was full of scrambled eggs and cheese and beans and slightly spicy sausage. Just what I needed right now. Drinking coffee on an empty stomach made me way too jittery. Or maybe that feeling could be blamed entirely on the kiss in the car.

"That's sweet," she said finally.

"I guess. It's also awkward when someone doesn't know her rules and then brings a side dish and she smiles and you can tell she's mad, but trying to hide it." I snorted. "No one in my family is good at hiding what they're thinking, except for maybe my dad, but he's the only mellow one, so he might just not have that strong emotions." Dad never really got worked up about anything, positive or negative. My sisters and I had competed to see who could get the biggest rise out of him.

Faith had won by getting engaged to a man she'd only been dating for two weeks. That had earned her raised eyebrows and slight concern. Mom had blown a gasket. My ears were still ringing from the yelling, and that had been years ago.

"You feel good about being around so many people?" I asked, just checking in one last time. Not only were my sisters loud, but they had produced loud children.

"I'll be fine," Ezra said, finishing her burrito and wiping her hands on a paper towel I'd handed her earlier.

"You will be fine," I said with more confidence than I felt. It wasn't Ezra that I was worried about, exactly. She seemed like she could hold her own. It was me I was worried about. The chances that my mother would see through this entire plot were high, and I was already mentally preparing myself for the fallout.

I couldn't finish my burrito, but I did drain the rest of my coffee.

"I should probably get going," Ezra said. "Put on something more respectable for meeting the family."

"Oh, you don't have to do that. We're not fancy people."

"Still," she said, glancing at the door. It didn't take a genius to see that she wanted to get away from me. Great. My fake wedding date was trying to escape me.

I fought back a sigh and nodded as I cleaned up from breakfast.

"I'll see you in a few hours," I said.

"Sounds good," she said as she paused by the door. She looked down at my mouth and then back up again. Was that indecisiveness in her eyes?

Ezra blinked once and then smiled at me.

"I'll see you later, Joy."

She tapped the frame of the door once before turning around and heading down the stairs. I blocked Clementine from following her as I watched her disappear from the doorway.

"What do you think, Clem? Is this going to blow up in my face?"

Clementine just rubbed his head against my leg and then meowed loudly.

∼

FOR THE FIRST TIME EVER, I was nervous about what to wear for dinner with my family. I tried on four different shirts before picking one that was nice but didn't look like I was trying too hard.

If I dressed up too much, my mom would know something was off and then her radar would be up.

I emerged from my room and rubbed my damp palms on my jeans. Why did they have to sweat so much when I was nervous? So embarrassing.

"Wow, you look nice," Sydney said, looking up from where she was sprawled on the couch with Clementine and a book.

"Do I?" I asked. "Nicer than usual?"

Sydney stared at me. "I'm not sure what answer you want."

"I don't want to look like I'm trying too hard, because my mom is basically Agatha Christie and she'll know I'm trying too hard if I dress up too much," I said.

Sydney sat up, dislodging a grumpy Clementine.

"Okay, you need to calm down a little, Joy," she said.

I sat down near her and groaned. "This was such a bad idea, Syd. What was I thinking? I should tell Ezra that I've changed my mind."

"Come on, Joy. This isn't that big of a deal. It's not like you murdered someone. You paid someone to be a date to your sister's wedding, who cares?"

"What would your mom say?" I asked.

Syd snorted. "She'd lose her goddamn mind."

"Exactly," I said. "Our moms are not calm, go-with-the-flow people."

I took a deep breath and Syd squeezed my shoulder.

There was a knock at the door, and it could only be one person.

"She's early," I said, getting to my feet on wobbly legs.

"Hey, don't stress out too much. It'll be fine," Sydney said before going back to her book.

"It will be fine," I repeated to myself and went to open the door.

"Hey," I said.

"Hey, sorry I'm early," Ezra said. Her hair was back in a smooth bun, and her striped shirt was crisp, as if she'd ironed it. She'd paired the shirt with a pair of clean black jeans (no holes) and dark red boots that were so new, they didn't have a scuff on them.

"You look great," I said, taking in her entire look.

"I assumed I should cover at least some of the tattoos. I never know how parents will react to them. Can't do much about these except wear thick rings. I have some, if you want me to wear them." She held up her hand and I shook my head. The urge to seize that hand and kiss those knuckles was so strong I could barely stand it.

"No, you don't have to do that. Two of my sisters have tattoos and so do their husbands."

"Good," she said, exhaling. "You look lovely, by the way."

"Thanks," I said, fighting the need to fidget in my clothes. "We should probably get going."

I grabbed my bag and we headed downstairs to my car. It took two tries to get my car started. I needed to get my act together on the drive.

As if she sensed my nerves, Ezra started asking me to go through my family members again. My sisters and their personalities and their husbands and children.

"The kids will probably ask you about the tattoos, so be prepared for that," I said.

"Of course. Kids ask all kinds of questions that adults also think, but aren't brave enough to say out loud," she said.

"It's true," I said. "And sometimes your niece tells you that she's sorry you're going to be dead by next year as she pats your cheek."

Ezra chuckled. "Has that happened to you?"

"Oh yeah. Kids will say all kinds of creepy things."

We arrived too soon at my parents; house. They'd downsized since all four of us girls left, so I didn't have a ton of emotional attachment to this house, but it was sweet and cozy, painted a cheery red with a bird feeder and a laundry line outside.

It looked like most of my sisters were already here, which was annoying. I was on time, but it seemed like I was late. We might be adults, but sometimes the competitiveness still came out in odd ways.

"Ready?" I said as I turned to Ezra. She was looking up at the house with something like apprehension.

"Ready," she said. "Stay right there."

Not sure what she meant, I waited as she got out of the car and walked around to open my door for me.

"It seemed like the right thing to do," she said, holding out her hand as if I was a celebrity getting out of a limo.

"Thank you," I said. "You didn't have to do that."

Ezra shrugged as we reached the front door and I opened it up.

"Mom!" I said, nearly crashing into my mother, who'd been standing right behind the door. Probably looking out to watch me get out of the car with Ezra.

I wanted to roll my eyes, but I didn't.

"Joy-Joy, so good to see you." She pulled me into a hug, but I was quickly discarded in favor of Ezra.

"Hello again, Ezra," she said. "Welcome to our home."

"It's nice to be here, Mrs. Greene."

"Oh please, call me Sarah. Calling me Mrs. Greene makes me feel old," she said with a laugh.

"You're not old, Mom," I said, but she was ignoring me. I shucked off my shoes and hung up my coat, reaching my hand out to take Ezra's.

Mom was saved from making any kind of witty reply by the arrival of the rest of my family.

"Joy-Joy! We haven't seen you in forever!" Faith exclaimed, pulling me into a hug.

"I've been busy," I said.

"You shouldn't be too busy for family," Mom said, giving my shoulder a squeeze that was a little painful. Emily was next to give me a hug, and Anna last, as if they'd lined up in birth order.

"This is Ezra," I said, gesturing to Ezra who waved.

"Hello, everyone," she said, her eye twitching slightly. All of us were crammed in the foyer, so she was really getting the full Greene family experience all at once.

"How about we move this into the living room?" Mom said, herding us all like a woman experienced in herding groups of people to where she wanted them.

The kids had been parked in front of the TV, but they jumped up to come over and hug me and then I was barraged with questions about Ezra.

She was still getting passed around and introduced to my sister's husbands, as well as Robert, Anna's fiancé. My dad was parked in his chair with a book, like a large stone in the middle of a rushing river.

I pulled Ezra from the chaos and dragged her over to him.

"Hi, Dad," I said, leaning down to give him a hug.

"Oh, Joy, I didn't see you come in." He blinked at me from behind his glasses.

"We were attacked by the welcoming committee. This is Ezra," I said.

"It's nice to meet you," Ezra said, looking unsure if she should hug him.

"Did you draw on your hands too?" a little voice said. Ezra and I looked down to find Paul, Faith's oldest looking at Ezra's hand with the tattoos on the knuckles.

He held up his hand, which was covered in faded marker streaks, as if he'd tried to wash them off and given up.

Ezra looked at me and then down at Paul.

"They're tattoos. It's like drawing with a permanent marker. They don't wash off," she said.

Paul looked up at Ezra with big eyes. "Prove it."

The audacity of this kid.

"She doesn't have to prove it, Paul," I said. "And what has your mom told you about being nice to guests?"

Paul completely ignored me and his interest seemed to draw all the other kids, including little Chloe, who crawled over to see what the fuss was about.

Ezra gave me a panicked look.

"Come on," I said, grabbing her hand.

"Where are you going?" Mom yelled from the kitchen.

"Bathroom!" I called back.

We couldn't all fit comfortably in the bathroom, but I squished the kids in and picked up little Rose so she could see what Ezra was going to do.

"Watch. She's going to put soap on her hands and the marks won't wash off," I said.

Ezra did so and the kids stared as she scrubbed, and the letters didn't come off.

"Now can anyone tell me what letter is on her pointer finger?" I asked.

"It's a L!" Paul yelled before anyone could have a chance to guess.

"That's right, it's an L. And what is the second letter?"

"O!" Paul yelled again.

"Okay, Paul, you really know your letters. How about we let Rosie or Talia guess?" I said, looking at the two girls. We'd left baby Chloe in the living room.

Rose and Talia were three and four, so I wasn't sure how good their grasp on letters was, but Talia yelled out "V!" and then we got to E.

"Paul, since you're the oldest, do you know what L-O-V-E spells?" I was pretty sure he didn't, but I knew he was going to want to be given the chance to try. He was five going on forty.

Paul furrowed his brow and I could tell he was really thinking it over.

"Would you like a hint?" I asked as he struggled. Rosie wiggled in my arms and I put her down.

"What does Mama say when she puts you to bed at night?" I asked.

"Goodnight, sleep tight," Paul said. "I don't know what that means."

I snorted and couldn't look at Ezra.

"Does she say anything else?"

"If I get scared, that I should use my monster spray," Paul said.

"Okay, does she say anything that begins with the letter L?"

Paul thought about that.

"What do you think Talia? I asked.

"I'm hungry," she said.

"So close," I said under my breath.

Rosie threw her arms around my legs. "Luff you, auntie," she said.

"Love!" Paul said. "Does it say love?"

"It does say love," Ezra said. She'd been silent this whole time, crammed in this bathroom with me and a bunch of kids.

"But why would you put love on your hand?" Paul asked, looking up at Ezra.

"So I don't forget that love exists in the world," Ezra said, gazing down at him.

Paul stared back up at Ezra.

We were all saved by Emily leaning in the doorway, Chloe on her hip.

"There you are. Talia, come wash up for dinner."

Talia skipped off and I lined the other kids up at the sink.

"I want a tattoo," Paul said as he dried his hands.

"You'll have to talk to your parents about that," I said.

"Why?" Paul asked.

"Because if you're under 18, you have to get permission to get a tattoo from your parents," I said.

His face lit up. "Okay! I'll just ask Santa!" He ran off and I heard Ezra laughing.

"He's a handful, that one," she said.

"They all are, believe me," I said, leaning against the wall. I wasn't ready to go out into the mayhem yet.

Ezra flicked her wrist and closed the door, which gave us a little privacy.

"Much better," I said, referencing the decrease in noise, but Ezra was looking at me as if I meant something entirely different.

"You doing okay?" I asked. Was it just me or was this bathroom getting smaller and smaller? There should be more space now that it was just the two of us, not less.

"You're sweet with them," Ezra said, leaning toward me.

"Thanks. They're fun, most of the time. It's nice to hand them to their parents when they get cranky."

"I've never been good with kids," Ezra said.

"What are you talking about? You were great with them."

"No, that was all you, Joy."

I opened my mouth to say something, but a tiny hand pounded on the door.

"Gotta pee pee!" a little voice yelled.

I held back a groan of frustration. "Guess it's time to go."

The little hand pounded again, and I opened the door to find Talia looking very suspicious.

"My turn," she said, shoving past me.

"Dinner's ready!" Mom yelled.

∼

SOMETIMES I WONDERED if there really were families where you could actually hear yourself think during dinner.

We were not that family. Even before my nieces and nephew arrived, even before my sisters got married, we were talking all over each other at once, having four or five different conversations.

Ezra sat next to me on one end of the second table that Mom had had to get when the family expanded. I tried to include her, but a lot of it went right over her head. Bits of gossip about people she didn't know, old stories she hadn't been present for. She was pretty quiet, but then I heard her say something to my dad and he answered her. They started talking about the weather, of all things. Dad talked about preparing for winter and how much work keeping the walk shoveled was. Ezra seemed interested, or at the very least she was pretending she was.

Figuring she was okay, I turned my attention back to Anna, who was on my other side, with Robert on her left.

"I've decided against speeches," Anna said.

"No speeches?" Mom said with a gasp. "What do you mean?"

Anna shared a look with Robert, and I noticed that he squeezed her hand under the table.

"I just don't think I need to hear anything like that at my wedding, or the rehearsal dinner. We thought that everyone could write down what they want to say in a card or a letter," Anna said, looking at Robert, who nodded. A man of few words was that Robert. Very similar to Dad.

Mom launched into a rant about how Anna needed to have speeches at her wedding, for some reason, and ended it with "but it's your wedding, so you can do what you want."

Anna's jaw was tight. Sure, it was her wedding, but Mom was going to get her opinion heard no matter what. My two other sisters had put up with the same song and dance and now it was her turn.

Moments like this were why I'd strongly considered eloping, if I ever got into a serious relationship with someone. Doing so might lead my mother to murder me and my new wife, but at least we would have gotten to have our own wedding our way.

Anna was saved from fighting further by one of the kids chucking a handful of potatoes at one of the other kids.

Ezra still seemed absorbed with talking to my father, so I didn't interfere and at last, the plates were empty, and it was time to carry them to the kitchen and see if we could make our exit.

Mom would want us to stay for dessert, but I wanted to get both me and Ezra out of here. She'd somehow escaped dinner relatively unscathed, which I hadn't anticipated. Normally, Mom would have honed right in on her and fired off the questions like bullets, but she'd been too busy harassing Anna about her wedding.

"We should probably get going," I said, touching Mom's shoulder.

"What for? We're just about to have coffee and I made a cherry pie. Your favorite. Even got chocolate ice cream to go with it," Mom said, as if that settled it. The pie was a draw, but my desire to get Ezra out before my family did anything really weird was stronger.

"Oh, that sounds great, but we really do have to get going—"

Mom interrupted me. "Joy. What could you possibly have to get home for on a Sunday evening? You can stay for dessert."

I glanced over at Ezra, who had moved into the living room with Dad. She couldn't save me. I'd had such grand plans of getting out of here, and then I was standing in front of my mother and she reduced me to a child.

I'd never been good at standing up to her, and this was no exception.

"Okay," I said, and she smiled and gave me a hug.

"That's my girl."

There could be worse things than being with your family and being force-fed pie.

Mom also roped me into helping take orders and bringing plates to people. The kids were starting to get cranky and tired, so Faith pulled out pillows and blankets for the living room floor, and she put on a soothing video. Most of the kids were going to crash before they even finished their dessert and would get carefully carried out to the car by their parents.

"Do you need any help?" Ezra asked, getting up when I came to her.

"If you don't mind?" I was frazzled and anxious, and I bet it was written all over my face.

"Not at all," Ezra said, excusing herself and following me into the kitchen. Mom was filling up the coffee pot again as the kettle whistled on the stove for anyone who wanted tea.

"Can you grab some cider for the kids?" Mom said. Anna and Robert were still dealing with the dinner dishes, and Faith and Emily were dealing with their offspring.

"Where is it?" Ezra asked as I searched for cups.

"Fridge. Top shelf," I said. Ezra got the cider and I found the kid's cups in a different cabinet than they should have been and we started filling them before taking plates of pie and utensils out as well.

I forgot the ice cream, so I had to go back and get that, but we eventually got the little ones set up with their treats and I was glad I didn't have to deal with the spills or wash the stained blankets.

At last Ezra and I got our pie and she declined ice cream but did put a little bit of whipped cream on top of her slice.

"I've never seen anyone eat cherry pie with chocolate ice cream," Ezra commented. We'd situated ourselves near Dad, which was the quieter side of the living room. I almost wish that my parents hadn't sold their other house, because there had been a huge finished basement with a little kitchen and bar and foosball table down there and it would have been just the right size for these family gatherings. Now the table lived in the garage.

"That's a shame, because it's the best combination there is. Except for maybe strawberries and chocolate," I said. "Cherries and chocolate just go together."

"I'll take your word for it," Ezra said, and she smiled. Warmth suffused my body, as if I'd drunk a few sips of wine.

There was a chance that this evening would turn out fine after all.

"So, Ezra, I didn't get a chance to ask you anything about yourself," my mother said, yanking a chair right over to sit in front of us.

So close.

Ezra chewed and swallowed, patting her mouth with her napkin.

"What do you want to know?" she asked, and I almost groaned.

"Well, we don't know much about you, now do we?" That was both a question and a threat.

Ezra didn't seem rattled at all. "There's not much to know. I'm not a very interesting person."

Mom laughed, and I could tell it was her fake laugh, and not the laugh of someone who was amused by something.

Great. This was just great.

"Oh, I wouldn't say that. And you seem very interested in my daughter."

I tried to keep eating my pie and ice cream like a normal person, but all I wanted to do was flee.

"That's correct. I am interested in her," Ezra said, meeting my eyes. That was definitely a lie, but I believed her. Well done.

"How long have you been seeing each other?" Mom's smile was sweet, but her question was sharp. A velvet-wrapped knife.

I looked to Ezra and she glanced at me before focusing her attention back on Mom.

"Just a few weeks. I don't normally meet the parents this early, but it seemed like the right thing to do," Ezra said.

"Going to a wedding together is pretty serious. Not something for a casual relationship," Mom said, not even pausing.

The hits kept on coming.

I pressed my damp palms to my jeans. Ezra reached over and took my hand, linking her fingers with mine.

I took a breath and the world seemed to settle a bit.

She squeezed my fingers and said, "I don't see this as a casual relationship."

It took every ounce of control I had to not look at her in surprise.

Mom's eyes flicked back and forth from me to Ezra and then she smiled slowly.

"Well, that's good to hear. Now, tell me about your family."

Ezra's grip tightened on mine for a moment. As if she was the one who needed reassurance. I squeezed back.

"We're not very close," she said.

"I'm sorry to hear that. Family is so important."

I clenched my teeth together to prevent me from saying anything.

"Sometimes you have to create your own family," Ezra said softly.

The tension kept getting thicker and I couldn't take it anymore.

I stood up abruptly, almost dumping my empty plate on the floor.

"We really should get going," I said, my hand still linked with Ezra's.

She looked up at me and I tried to communicate that we should get out now.

"We should," Ezra said, standing up with me. "Thank you so much for dinner."

Ezra briefly let go of my hand and turned to Mom. She

stood up and held her arms out. We both hugged her, and I leaned down to give Dad a hug. His eyes were drooping, and I knew he was going to fall asleep in his chair.

"Let me walk you out," Mom said, putting her hand on my lower back. I moved away and reached out until I found Ezra's hand again.

I pressed myself into her and she guided me toward the front door and got both our coats for us. She even helped me on with mine as Mom chattered about when we could come for dinner again.

"We'll let you know," I said, startling even myself by the use of "we." Like Ezra and I were a unit.

"Okay," Mom said, hugging me again. "Don't be a stranger."

"I won't," I said.

"And call me back," she said.

"I will," I said, suddenly so tired I could fall asleep right in the middle of the floor.

"Thank you for a lovely evening," Ezra said, finally breaking in and pulling me toward the door.

There was a chorus of goodbyes and then we were walking toward the car and I was trying not to cry.

∼

IT WASN'T until I was driving away from the house that I took a true deep breath.

"Fuck," I said. "I'm so sorry. I know I warned you."

Ezra reached over and stroked my shoulder. "Hey, it's okay. It's not your fault. You can't choose your parents. It wasn't that bad."

"She just thinks that she can say whatever she wants to people and Dad doesn't call her out. I don't call her out and I know I should, but I feel like a little kid again every time I try."

My fingers gripped the steering wheel until they ached.

"I prepare all these speeches and practice them and then I get in front of her and I forget everything. And it's not like she's doing anything bad! She doesn't scream at me or say anything truly mean, but it still feels like shit."

Once I started, I couldn't stop. I even pulled into the parking space behind my apartment and kept going. Ezra sat sideways in the passenger seat so she was facing me, her face illuminated under the orange glow of the streetlight.

"I'm sorry. You did not sign up for this," I said when I finally stopped.

"Joy," she said. "It's okay. You don't have to apologize to me."

I leaned forward, resting my head on the steering wheel. "You don't have to return the money."

"What?" she said. My voice had been muffled.

"I said that you don't have to return the money."

She looked at me in confusion.

"I'm sure you are ready to bail now. You don't have to be my wedding date. But you came to my parent's dinner, so you don't have to return the first payment. I'll tell my family that we had a fight."

This time Ezra grabbed my hand and held it in both of hers.

"Joy. I'm not running."

I blinked at her. "What?"

"I'm not bailing on you. I'll still be your wedding date. I've been through far worse dinners, most with my own family. I'm not that fragile that your mom is going to scare me off."

She smiled and leaned toward me. "I think your mom has good intentions, I really do. Her social skills and boundaries definitely need some work, though."

I snorted. That was an understatement.

"She's not used to anyone standing up to her," I said.

"I can see that," Ezra said, her thumb moving in soothing circles on the back of my hand.

"I hope Anna decides to do what she wants with her wedding. One of us should. Remind me to tell you about Faith's and Emily's weddings. Mom hijacked both of them and it was easier to let her have her way. Like she's a cranky toddler."

It sounded so silly when I said it out loud. All of us bending to her will so she wouldn't be upset.

"She has the advantage of knowing what to say to get things to be her way," Ezra said.

"I know," I said, looking down at my hand in hers. The dark lines of her knuckle tattoos were visible, even in the low light.

"You probably have better things to do than listen to me complain about my family," I said.

"Hey," Ezra said, squeezing my hand. "I'm fine right where I am."

I was about to say something else when my phone went off. Ezra released her grip on my hand, and I saw I had a message from Sydney.

"It's just Syd. She's wondering how things went." I said that I was on my way home, but not that I was already here.

"Thanks for tonight," I said.

"Of course," Ezra said. "What are fake dates for?"

She smiled and I found myself smiling back.

"I'll let you get back to your life. Our next event isn't until the bridal shower in two weeks, so you are free to forget me and my family exist."

I didn't want to pressure Ezra to feel like she had to spend a lot of time with me. She was only obligated for a few events, and I didn't want to be greedy.

"I think we should have another practice session, don't you?" Ezra said after a pause.

"Another practice session?"

She nodded. "You know, to keep up appearances."

"You don't have to—"

Ezra put one finger to my lips. "Joy. If you don't want to spend time with me, just say so."

I wanted to lick her finger so bad, and the urge came out of the blue, but I clamped my teeth down on my tongue so I wouldn't. Finger licking definitely wasn't part of the deal.

Ezra removed her finger.

"I do want to spend time with you. I just didn't want you to feel obligated."

"Do I look like the kind of person who does things out of obligation?" she countered.

"I guess not," I said.

"I'd like to spend time with you, Joy. If you want."

I did. I did want. I wanted so much that I ached from it.

"Okay, uh, what did you have in mind?" I asked.

"How about I come visit you at the bookstore tomorrow on your break and we can talk about it?" she said.

"That sounds good." She wanted to see me tomorrow. That was good. I'd fully expected her to renege on this deal after meeting my parents. Well, my mom specifically.

"Go debrief with Sydney," she said, nodding up at the apartment. She pushed the door open and I heard the jingle of keys.

I wished there were a reason to ask her to come upstairs. I also wished I didn't have a nosy roommate.

"No one died, so I call that a win," Ezra said, swinging her keys around one of her fingers as she leaned on my bumper.

"I guess so," I said, laughing a little.

"Tomorrow is always another day," she said.

"With no mistakes in it," I said, paraphrasing Anne Shirley. I wondered if Ezra had read those books. They were among some of my absolute favorites and the first books I really escaped into when I was younger and longing for an escape from the chaos of my family.

"That's right," Ezra said, pushing off the car. "Have a good night, Joy."

"You too," I said, and she unlocked her car and got it. I waited until she started the engine and pulled out before I went upstairs.

Chapter Seven

"How did it go?" Sydney said from the couch. She was in the exact same position I'd left her in earlier.

"It was awful, but Ezra didn't back out, so I guess it couldn't have been that terrible," I said, hanging up my bag and setting my keys in the little pottery bowl by the door that Sydney's mom painted.

Sydney closed her book and got up. "You look like you definitely need a hug."

I did, so I put my arms out and she enveloped me, and I breathed in her familiar scent of rose body oil.

Sydney leaned back and looked at me. "You want to talk?"

"No, I'm good. I already dumped everything on Ezra during the ride back." I made a face, remembering.

"But she said that she's still cool with being your date?" Syd asked and we went over to the couch. I sat down and pulled one of the blankets around my shoulders for comfort, even though the apartment was warm.

"Yeah. She really is so chill about everything. I guess she has her own family issues, so mine don't seem like that bad," I said.

"You said she's not in contact with them, right?" Syd said, getting up and filling the kettle to make some tea. We'd done this ritual so many times together that it was automatic. One of us would need support and the other one would make some tea as we talked about it.

"Yeah. Reading between the lines, I think it was pretty bad. I don't have any details, but I can imagine they're awful." I shuddered.

"That's brutal," Sydney said, pulling down two mugs and then getting out the honey.

"I know. I try not to be too nosy about it because she clearly doesn't want to talk about it."

The kettle whistled and Sydney poured the tea and brought it over. Clementine woke up and meowed at me as if I'd been the one who disturbed his slumber.

"You woke yourself up, you dork," I told him. He yawned and closed his eyes again.

Sydney handed me the warm mug, yet another item formed and painted by her mother's hands.

"So how bad was your mom?" she asked, and I sighed.

"She was all over Anna about her wedding," I said. "Anna said no speeches and Mom is taking issue with that."

Syd made a face. "I think Anna should have her wedding however she wants, but I know my opinion doesn't count."

"According to my mom, Anna's opinion, and that of her fiancé, don't matter much either."

~

THE NEXT DAY WAS BUSY, since the local schools were out. Parents were desperate for something to do, so they piled into the bookstore. It was just me and Erin, the only other employee. She worked part time, and I was thrilled that we got along. As a mom of two, she was also excellent at knowing which books were popular with the kids, which was one of my weakest areas, in spite of being an aunt. She had an instinct about which books were going to land with kids that was almost supernatural. The Children's Story Hour was also her domain, and I was more than happy to let her take charge of that every week.

"I feel like I've been running a marathon," she said, smiling at me as another group of happy customers left the shop. The mid-afternoon lull was in the air and we were both grateful for the break.

"I know," I said as we tag-teamed the area in the back with the toys that looked like a tornado had swept through. Erin went through the stuffed toys and tucked them back on their shelves or in their basket and I reset the toy display.

"Excuse me, I was hoping you could help me find a book," a voice said, and I froze in the act of straightening a little wooden boat.

"Do you think you could help me?" I could hear her amusement and she had a smile on her face when I turned around.

"Hey," I said. "I think I can help you with that."

"I've got this," Erin said. I hadn't told her about Ezra, but I was sure she knew at least a little bit of the situation from talking to Kendra and other people who knew me.

Ezra moved over to the romance shelves.

"What kind of a book are you looking for?" I asked.

"Pick one for me," she said.

"I'd like some parameters," I said. "Picking the right book for the right reader is an art and the more I know, the better I can target a recommendation."

Sure, you could go online and let an algorithm do it for you, but there was something about having a person select a book that was just for you. When I was a child and I'd go to the library and ask the librarian to find me a book, it felt like magic when she'd press one into my hand that was exactly what I needed.

"Use your instincts," Ezra said. "I trust you."

I took a deep breath and looked at the shelves. This was a big ask. What if I chose wrong?

My fingers slipped along the spines and then I knew exactly what book to give her. I moved one shelf over and found several copies.

"This one," I said, presenting her the slim volume with a red and a blue bird on the cover.

"What's it about?" Ezra asked, taking it from me.

"Just read it," I said. "Isn't that what you do? Go into a book with no idea of what's going to happen?"

"You remember," she said.

"I mean, it wasn't that long ago, and it was pretty memorable, considering I propositioned you as my paid wedding date," I said. Ezra looked down at the cover.

"It was a memorable day," she said, turning the book over in her hands.

"Did you want anything else?" I asked, realizing I'd been drawing closer and closer to her.

"I want a lot of things, Joy," she said, and I wasn't sure what she meant.

"If those things are books, I can definitely help with that," I said.

Ezra took a step back. "If only they were all books."

We seemed to be having two different conversations.

"Life would be so simple," I said.

"Wouldn't it?"

Ezra's phone went off and she pulled it out of her pocket to look at the screen. "What are you doing after work?"

"Oh, um, just having dinner with Syd as usual. Nothing exciting." Part of me wanted to invite her. I liked the idea of

Ezra sitting with me and Sydney and eating something I'd cooked for her.

"Want to get a drink after? I promise not to keep you out too late," she said.

Getting a drink with Ezra sounded so adult. I'd never done something like that.

"Oh, sure. Did you have anyplace in mind?" We'd have to head out of Arrowbridge. The only places that served alcohol were a few of the restaurants and they didn't stay open past nine.

"I was wandering around and found this place in Castleton, Pine something," she said.

"Pine State Bar and Grille?" I asked.

"That's the one. Seemed like a cute place."

"I know the bartender, Esme and her wife. She's great. If you think I'm good with book recommendations, Esme is a genius when it comes to drinks. She'll just make something up on the spot that's exactly what you didn't know you wanted."

Ezra nodded at me and then walked toward the checkout counter. I followed her and scanned the book so she could pay.

"So I'll pick you up around nine?" Ezra asked.

I handed the book back to her with a receipt. She took it from me and winked.

I almost slid to the floor.

"Uh yeah," I managed to say.

"See you later, Joy," she said, leaving me weak in the knees.

A voice behind me made me jump. "Who was that?"

I put my hand on my leaping heart and turned to find Erin staring at the door.

"Oh. That's Ezra," I said. Seemed as good an explanation as any.

"The one who's going to your sister's wedding?" she asked.

"Uh huh."

"Wow," Erin said. "I know I'm straight and everything, but then I sometimes reconsider."

"Curiosity is always encouraged," I said, bumping my shoulder with hers.

"There's something about her, isn't there?" Erin said, shaking herself.

"Oh, there is," I said.

∽

"LOOK AT YOU, having drinks with your fake date. Are we calling her your fake girlfriend?" Sydney said as we ate dinner.

"I don't know," I said. "We haven't talked about it."

"You probably should," Syd said as she poked a potato onto her fork.

"Yeah." There were a lot of things that Ezra and I hadn't talked about. I seemed to forget everything important whenever she was around. It was starting to be a problem.

"Is this like a date? Like a real date?" Syd said.

"No. It's just getting drinks," I said.

"Getting drinks is usually a date, Joy."

"Under normal circumstances, but I don't think it counts. I told her she didn't have to spend time with me outside of our paid events, but she said she wanted to, so I have no idea what's going on and I'm trying to not think about it too much."

Ezra was still a complete stranger to me, and her motives were a mystery.

"I'm going to say something that you're not going to believe but, Joy, I think she likes you."

Sydney put down her fork and turned to look at me.

"I think she likes hanging out with me, but there's nothing to it more than that," I said, and Sydney rolled her eyes.

"You know, for a smart person, you can be an idiot sometimes. Have you ever considered that she likes you in a real way? And that she agreed to be your date because she wanted to get close to you?"

I stared at Sydney.

"Then why ask me for money?"

"To throw you off. To make you believe that she was just doing it for cash," Syd said.

I threw my hands in the air. "That doesn't make any sense!"

"People don't make sense a lot of the time," Syd said. "I know I don't understand a lot of people."

"No, that's way too convoluted," I said. "The simplest explanation is she might be trying to scam me for more money."

Sydney made a frustrated sound.

"Being your friend is really a difficult job sometimes, Joy. You are an awesome person. Why is it easier to believe that someone would be scamming you than that they'd have a crush on you?"

I opened my mouth to answer her, but I didn't really have a good answer.

"Because," I said.

Syd got up and took her plate to the sink. "That's a very mature response, Joy. I don't get it. You're literally the most romantic person I know, so why don't you think it could happen for you?"

It was a good question.

"I do think it could happen for me," I said. "Just not like this."

"Why not?"

"Because it's just not realistic."

Syd crossed her arms. "Now you're not making sense. You know what I think?"

She was going to tell me whether I wanted to hear it or not.

"I think you're scared. You're scared that reality and your

fantasy of this perfect love won't match, or that you might be disappointed."

I stood up even though I hadn't finished eating.

"I don't want to talk about this anymore," I said, dumping the rest of my dinner in the trash and cramming my plate in the dishwasher.

"Joy," Sydney said, her voice soft. A hand touched my shoulder.

"I said I didn't want to talk about this anymore," I repeated.

To her credit, Syd didn't push. She could be confrontational, but she could also be soft.

"Okay," she said. "Did you want to watch that new episode?"

"Sure," I said, grateful that she'd changed the subject.

∽

AS THE TIME for my drink with Ezra drew closer, I got more and more anxious. What did it mean? I wished I was brave like Sydney, who would have come right out and asked her.

I wasn't really brave. Asking Ezra to be my wedding date was an anomaly that I still didn't really understand.

"What did that blanket ever do to you?" Syd said, and I realized I'd been pulling at the threads of the blanket on my lap. It was one I'd made myself when I'd gotten a crochet kit from Layne one Christmas. I hadn't kept up the hobby, but I did want to go back to it. There was something so soothing about watching balls of yarn turning into a blanket or a scarf.

One minute before nine, there was a knock at the door. Ezra was always prompt.

I stood up and folded up the blanket again before I answered the door. Since I had no idea what kind of outfit was appropriate for drinks with your fake wedding date, I'd kept it casual with a pair of jeans and my favorite boots and a leather jacket that Sydney had made me buy when we'd been shopping once.

"Hey, I like the jacket," she said. A leather jacket would look much better on her, but that was kind of true of everything. She sported another flannel shirt and faded jeans with boots that almost matched the vibe of my jacket.

"Thanks. I like...all of this," I said, motioning to her outfit. She laughed softly.

"Ready to go?"

"Yup," I said, grabbing my bag.

"Have her home by midnight!" Sydney called from the couch.

"Will do," Ezra called back.

"If anything happens to her, I know at least five good places to hide a body," Sydney yelled.

"Okay, that's enough of that," I said, shoving Ezra out the door. At least she was laughing as we walked down the stairs and out to her car.

"Do you want me to drive?" I asked.

"No need. I'm not planning on having any alcohol," she said, and I wanted to ask if she was sober, but it seemed rude.

Ezra's car was surprisingly clean and smelled like it had just come from the dealership. It made me feel a little guilty about how much of a mess my car was. I could never seem to throw away all the disposable coffee cups that collected on the floor of the backseat.

"How was the rest of your day?" Ezra asked, and I told her about how I'd caught a kid trying to steal a book.

"I felt bad busting him to his parents, but he returned it and said he was sorry. His mom had no idea why he tried to do it, since she would have bought it for him."

"You never know what goes through someone else's mind sometimes," Ezra said.

"Isn't that the truth?" Most of the time I had no idea what was going through her mind.

"So if you don't drink, why did you suggest going to a bar?" I asked.

Ezra lifted one shoulder in a shrug. "I like bars. I've visited a lot of them everywhere. They're one of the first places I seek out when I go somewhere new."

"Where's your favorite bar?" I asked. Maybe now I could gain a little insight into who she was before she'd come to Arrowbridge.

"I love Howl, in Boston. I always try to seek out gay or lesbian bars when I can, and it's one of the best."

There was a lesbian bar I'd heard about that was about an hour away from Arrowbridge, but I'd never gone there.

"I heard a rumor someone wanted to build one in Arrowbridge, but I don't know if that's true or not," I said. The rumor had filtered from Sadie to Layne to me, and I had admit it was exciting to think about.

"There are a lot of queer people in Arrowbridge," Ezra said. "It's one of the reasons I came here. It was on a list of queer-friendly small towns."

I didn't know about that distinction, but it sounded about right.

"It didn't used to be, I don't think," I said. "I didn't grow up here, but Sydney did and she said it wasn't always rainbow-flag town."

"It's nice to see," Ezra said.

"There are a lot in Castleton too," I said. "I can introduce you to Esme if she's working. She'll make you a mocktail that will blow your socks off."

Ezra chuckled. "My socks are ready to be blown."

I laughed myself. It was such a dorky comment.

We pulled into the parking lot, which was only one-third

filled, but the music coming from the bar was loud, and the seats were almost filled.

"Is it always like this?" Ezra asked, leaning down to speak in my ear.

"Most nights, I think," I said. "Any port in a storm."

She nodded and we found two stools at the end of the bar. Esme was working, I was glad to see, and she smiled when I waved at her.

"Nice to see you down this neck of the woods. What can I get you?" She grinned at Ezra with her charming bartender smile.

"I'm going to have that cherry thing you made me last time, and Ezra will have…" I said, trailing off to give her an opening.

"Just a soda," Ezra said, and Esme leaned on the bar and studied her for a second.

"Are you up for a surprise drink? I want to try out a new mocktail."

Ezra glanced at me and then back at Esme. "Sure?"

Esme slapped the bar. "That's the spirit. Be right back."

Ezra looked around and took in the bar. "I like this place."

"It's cool. They have karaoke every week, but I've always avoided it. I'm not a karaoke kind of girl," I said.

She tilted her head as she focused on me again. "That surprises me. You look like you might like to get up there and belt it."

I shook my head as I shuddered. "No way. I don't want everyone staring at me. I'd get Sydney to go up. She has no shame and doesn't care."

Sydney would do karaoke naked if she wouldn't get arrested.

"She sounds like a lot," Ezra said and that made me laugh.

"Oh, she is. But I love her. And then there's Layne, who is like our friend mom. Always making sure we're fed and happy and she kisses our boo boos when we get hurt." You could always count on Layne take charge in a crisis, or to have a bandage or aspirin in her purse.

"Seems like you've built your own little family," she said.

"Yeah, I feel like I have. I know Syd and Layne are my best friends, but they feel more like sisters. I talk to them way more than my biological sisters. I know I should probably feel bad about that, but I don't."

I shrugged and Esme returned with our drinks.

"One Cherry Carrie and one Drink I Haven't Named Yet. Maybe I could name it after you, if you don't hate it."

I grabbed my drink and sipped it immediately. It was like the adult version of a Shirley Temple with a kick and I loved it.

Ezra picked up hers as if it was going to bite her. The drink was a dark red in color, and I was hoping that Ezra would give me a sip.

"What's in it?" she asked.

"Do you have any allergies?" Esme said, wiping the counter. "I should have asked."

Ezra shook her head.

"What happened to the woman who bought a book without reading the back cover?" I asked, and Ezra looked at me and smiled before taking a sip of the drink and looking up at the ceiling as she tasted it.

"What do you think?" I asked. Esme had to tend to other customers, so she wasn't there to see if Ezra liked the drink.

"It's good. Really good. Want to try?" She pushed the glass at me and I pulled the straw out of my drink and stuck it in hers. I took a generous sip.

"Ohh, that's good," I said. The drink was fruity, maybe blackberry? But it also had an herby taste that I couldn't identify.

"It is," Ezra said as I removed my straw. "It's nice to be able to get a decent drink that doesn't have alcohol."

I decided to go for it. "Are you sober?"

Ezra shook her head. "Not exactly. I just don't really like alcohol so I don't drink it. I hate the way it makes me feel."

That made sense. I was much more of a social drinker myself. Esme breezed over during a lull to find out if Ezra liked the drink.

"What is that herby taste?" I asked.

"Sage," Esme said. "I've been experimenting a lot with using herbs in my mocktails to give a new depth of flavor. Let me know if there's any changes I should make."

"I don't think so. It's perfect," Ezra said, and I saw that she'd almost finished it.

"Best compliment I can get," Esme said. "It's officially yours." She looked at me expectantly and I realized I hadn't introduced Ezra yet.

"Oh, sorry, Esme, this is Ezra," I said, not adding anything else. She and I still hadn't talked about definitions or labels or anything.

"Nice to meet you, Ezra," Esme said, sticking out her hand.

"Nice to meet you. Joy's told me you're the go-to bartender around here."

Esme smiled. "That's me. Well, it's great to meet you," she said, her eyes flicking over to where a rowdy group had just walked in.

"We'll let you get back to work. Say hi to Paige for me," I said. Esme winked before she went to serve the group.

"Her wife is pregnant right now. I think she's due soon," I said. I'd met Paige and Esme through Kendra. The threads that tied the queer community together here were many. There was that joke about everyone in small towns knowing each other, but it was even more true for queer people in small towns. We clung to each other, like barnacles on a rock so we had each other when we got slammed by the ocean.

Ezra leaned her head on her hand as she finished her drink.

"What are you thinking about?" I asked.

"I'm thinking that I picked the right place to move," she said. "There's something different about the air here. I'm probably just imagining it."

"No, you're not. I know I grew up in Maine, but I went away for college and then came back and never really felt the need to go anywhere else. People think that I just stayed for my family, but it would be much easier to live far away," I said with a laugh.

"Distance can be good when it comes to family," she said.

"Are you ever going to tell me about yours? I mean, you don't have to, but if you needed to, I wanted you to know that's okay. That I'd listen." I babbled away like a dumbass, but Ezra didn't laugh at me.

"Thanks. That's nice to hear. Most of the time I try not to think about it at all," she said. "I know that's probably not healthy, but my coping mechanisms have worked out great for me so far."

She flashed me a rueful smile.

"Here's to coping mechanisms," I said, raising my drink. Hers was almost gone, but she tapped her glass against mine anyway.

"Okay, enough about that. How about you tell me what you were like in school," I said. That was a pretty neutral question, I thought.

"I'd rather talk about what you were like in school," Ezra said, turning on that charming smile. It still hit me like a truck, but now that I'd spent a little bit of time with her, I could see what she was trying to do.

"I asked you first," I said, pointing at her. "Should I guess?"

Ezra laughed softly. "Go ahead."

"I bet…you were the coolest girl in school. Everyone

wanted to be you. I bet you didn't do any activities because you decided they were uncool. I bet you got good grades, but not too good to be noticed," I said. "How did I do?"

Ezra threw her head back and laughed. "Is that really what you think of me?"

"I don't know, you haven't given me enough to make an accurate assessment!" I said. "What was I wrong about?"

"I was in theater. And band. I had two friends and graduated salutatorian. That bitch Casey Kelley beat me by a fraction of a point and I'll never forget it."

Whoa. This was more personal information than I'd ever gotten before. I knew her drink didn't have alcohol in it, but Ezra seemed comfortable here, in this bar. In this environment.

I was glad she'd asked me to come.

"I've got to know what instrument you played," I said. That was the first of many, many questions.

Ezra sighed before she answered. "Trombone."

"Trombone?" my shriek was absorbed by the loudness of the bar. "You played the trombone?"

Ezra looked away from me and I could swear she was blushing under the light of a neon beer sign.

"Yes, I played the trombone. For seven years. Let me tell you, not the sexiest instrument," she said.

"I think that trombones can be very sexy," I said, trying to keep a straight face.

Ezra hit my shoulder lightly. "Shut up. And what were you like? Prom queen, no doubt."

I rolled my eyes. "Hardly. Two of my sisters were, though, and I never heard the end of it. No matter what I did, one of my sisters had done it first. I nearly drove myself insane trying to keep up and be better, but I never got there. It wasn't until I graduated from college that I gave up and decided to do my own thing."

"Are you doing your own thing now?" she asked.

I nodded. "Yeah. And let me tell you, being a bookseller is not what Mom had in mind for me and she doesn't let me forget it. She drops little digs here and there."

I sighed. I didn't want to talk about my mom.

"So, if you were in theater, does that include musical theater? Does that include you getting on stage and singing?" I asked, turning the tables back on Ezra.

Her lips pressed together before she admitted, "Yes."

"Favorite role," I fired at her.

"Fantine in Les Mis," she said without hesitation.

"Obviously," I said.

"Obviously," she agreed.

"Now, is there evidence of this performance? Perhaps an online recording?"

Ezra's eyes narrowed. "I will admit to nothing."

"That means there is, if I want to put in the work to find it," I said.

Ezra made a groaning noise. "I shouldn't have told you that. Bars make me chatty, apparently."

"I like chatty Ezra. She's fun."

She pretended to be offended. "I'm always fun."

"When was the last time you did something fun?" I asked.

Ezra leaned closer and dropped her voice. "I'm doing something fun right now."

"Oh, so this is fun?" I asked, also leaning, drawn completely into her.

"Being with you is fun, Joy," she said, and even though her voice was soft, I could hear it over all the other noise.

"You should have more fun in your life, then," I said.

"Will you help me?" she asked.

"Help you be more fun?" I asked.

"Mmmhmm."

"Are you gonna pay me?"

Ezra grinned. "I was hoping you'd do it out of the goodness of your heart."

I scoffed. "Oh, I see how it is. I need something and have to come up with the cash, but you need me and suddenly you want free labor."

"How about this? How about I foot the bill for all our fun and agree to drive. Is that a fair exchange?"

I had to admit, that sounded an awful lot like dating.

"So this is just me teaching you to have fun, and nothing else?" I asked.

"Just fun, nothing else," she agreed.

"I'm in," I said. "As long as it doesn't interfere with our previous arrangement."

"Of course, that takes precedence," she said, nodding gravely.

Esme came over and handed Ezra another drink without her even having to ask.

"To fun," Ezra said.

"To fun."

∼

I DECIDED NOT to have a second drink, but Ezra finished hers and we talked more about growing up. I gave her a taste of what growing up with three older sisters was like and she told me about her two best friends from school, Joel and Alex.

"We were less the Three Musketeers and more the Three Weirdos," she said.

"Oh come on, you probably weren't that weird."

"I wore black lipstick all of junior year and wore a pentagram around my neck. A few of the more conservative parents even had a meeting about me casting spells on their children."

I almost choked on the water that Esme had brought me.

"You've got to be kidding," I said.

"I grew up in Massachusetts," she said. "Home of the Salem Witch Trials."

Right.

"Are there pictures?" I asked.

"None that you're going to get to see." She'd smiled so much tonight. It was beautiful to see.

I pouted. "Not even one?"

Her smile froze and she sat back, just a little. I'd moved so far forward that I was almost in her lap and my stool kept tipping.

"Don't you pout at me," she said.

"Why not?"

Even though I'd only had one drink, I was feeling pretty flirtatious.

Ezra pressed her lips together and looked away from me. "It's getting late."

Was it? I'd lost all track of time and was shocked when I checked the clock on my phone.

"Oh crap, it is late."

Ezra motioned to Esme and then handed over her card to close out the tab.

"I'm paying for the fun, remember?" she said.

"Right," I said, my mood sinking to the sticky floor as I hopped off the stool and headed for the door.

The magic of our little bar bubble had burst, and I didn't know if I'd ever be back in that place again. That place that felt like it existed just for the two of us.

"You okay?" Ezra asked as we got in the car.

"Yeah," I said. "Just thinking."

"Anything in particular?" she asked.

I decided to lie. "Just that next time I go to the bar, I'm going to order myself an Ezrahito," I said.

She let out a surprised snort. "It's not going to be called that."

"Why not?"

"Absolutely not," she said.

"Okay, what are your suggestions?" I asked.

"No puns with my name. They feel like a gimmick. I'll think about it and get back to you. It has to feel right."

"You're taking this drink naming very seriously," I said.

"It's important. I don't want to be known for a drink called Butthole Bomb or something," she said.

I wheezed out a laugh. "Butthole Bomb? Who would create or drink something called that?" I couldn't stop laughing. For some reason it was one of the funniest things I'd ever heard.

Ezra laughed too, as I wiped tears from my eyes.

"I'm sure someone somewhere has created a drink called Butthole Bomb and they have a special toast that they say when they drink it."

I was sure there probably was. There was always someone out there doing something inexplicable.

We arrived back at my apartment still laughing as we came up with more and more ridiculous drink names.

"I can't stop laughing," I said, holding my hurting stomach.

"I'm not sorry," Ezra said, turning her car off. "You have a great laugh, Joy."

The air in the car changed and I looked over at her.

"Thanks," I said.

Ezra inhaled through her nose and looked out the windshield at a sign that said TENANT PARKING ONLY, VIOLATORS WILL BE TOWED.

"I should let you get to bed," she said.

"Someone's gotta sell the books," I said.

"Mmm," she said, and I could see that I'd lost her again. Where did she go?

"Okay, well let me know if you need any more fun. I don't

have your number," I said. We'd still been communicating via email.

"What's yours?" Ezra asked, taking out her phone. I told her and she typed it into hers and then sent me a message.

It's Ezra the message said.

Hi Ezra I typed back and sent. She let out a soft laugh and looked up at me.

"I'll let you know if I need fun," she said. "Goodnight."

"Goodnight, Ezra," I said. Saying her name felt decadent for some reason. I savored it.

I got out of the car and waited again for her to leave before I went upstairs.

Chapter Eight

I couldn't stop myself from checking my phone a million times the next day, hoping for a message from Ezra that she needed emergency fun.

"Everything okay?" Kendra asked me. We were working on a display of new releases. "You keep checking your phone."

"Oh, yeah," I said, sliding it back in my pocket after checking to make sure all the alert noises were on.

"Waiting for a message from someone special? Someone with tattoos?" she asked, giving me a significant look.

There was no point in lying.

"Maybe," I said.

"Ohhh, so things are getting kind of real, I see," she said, bumping my hip with hers. I added another book to a pile and made sure the spines lined up.

"I wouldn't go that far. I still know practically nothing about her. She's not making it easy to get to know her," I said.

"Some people are like that. I can't seem to ever shut up, and then Theo can have a whole conversation with someone with one-word answers. It's amazing."

"Ezra doesn't even do that. She turns the conversation around and before you know it, she's the one asking all the questions and you're just answering them."

"Sounds exhausting," Kendra said.

"It's not. I think I'm making her sound bad. It's not that she's being manipulative, exactly. She's just very private and doesn't like invasive questions."

"How invasive are we talking?"

Kendra had a point. A lot of the questions I had for Ezra were basic and she danced around them like a champion tapper.

"She's a mystery. A mystery that I'm determined to figure out," I said.

"Mystery is sexy. Just be careful," she said.

"I always am," I said, handing her another book.

∽

EZRA DIDN'T CONTACT me for the next few days, so I kept myself busy by cooking elaborate dinners for Sydney and hanging out with Layne whenever I could and putting my effort into planning the next book club night.

The Mainely Books Club met once a month and discussed a book that we all voted on and sipped on wine (or juice) and actually did talk about the book before we moved on to town gossip. Another bonus of the club was that the majority of the members were queer, or at least queer-friendly, or queer-adjacent. Our picks were almost always queer, and it was a great way to support authors that might not normally get selected.

When I had the time, I would sit down with Kendra and plan out the book club meetings and do drinks and snacks and sometimes even a theme with decorations.

This month's pick was a sweet and fun romance about two

queer Black women who went on a marriage reality show and accidentally fell in love.

Since marriage was a big theme of the book, I went to a party store in a larger town and found all kinds of fun stuff. I even called up my favorite bakery in Castleton, Sweet's Sweets, and commissioned a small wedding cake and cupcakes for everyone to have. Linley wasn't part of the greater queer community, but her best friends were, so she was an honorary member as far as I was concerned. She and her husband were absolutely lovely and had the cutest little baby girl.

When I'd asked Linley if she could match the cake to the cover of the book, she said that was no problem. I couldn't wait for book club to meet so I could show everyone the cake.

"No Ezra?" Sydney asked me every night when I got home from work.

"Nope, nothing," I said. I was really trying not to be too disappointed, but I couldn't help myself. We'd had this incredible night at the bar and then she went radio silent.

The closer we got to all of the wedding activities, the worse my fear that she would back out, and her disappearing act didn't help.

"You gotta find out where she works," Sydney said, on Thursday night. Layne was leaving Honor to have dinner with her sister, Lark, and coming to see us solo.

I didn't resent Layne being in love, but it was nice to see her on her own. Those times were a lot fewer since she and Honor had gotten together. I missed her. We saw a lot more of each other in the summer when the twins were out of school and Layne would add a trip to the bookstore to their activities for the day.

"I come bearing gifts," Layne announced as she walked through the door. She had a key, and she never needed to knock.

Clementine ran over to investigate, hoping she would have treats, but he was sorely disappointed when she let him sniff the container.

"Not for you, I'm afraid," Layne said before setting it on the counter and giving me a hug. She smelled like chocolate, which was what I hoping was what she'd brought. Along with herself, of course.

"Edible gifts?" Sydney said, hugging Layne and then going to peel the lid of the container.

"The twins and I made three different kinds of fudge the other day when they were home from school, so I saved you some," she said.

"Wait," Sydney said, holding up one hand. "You supervised them, right?"

"Of course. I wouldn't feed you anything I wouldn't eat myself. Besides, they're almost twelve. It's not like they're adding boogers. Anymore."

I had to stop myself from gagging. "Subject change, please."

"Who wants tea?" Sydney said, and I raised my hand, along with Layne.

She leaned down to give Clementine some love before we all camped on the couch with tea and fudge.

"Oh my god, this is amazing," Sydney said through a mouthful.

"I'm glad you like it. There's double chocolate cherry for Joy, and then rainbow cereal milk, and then chocolate peanut butter fudge, which the twins decided on."

It didn't matter that the amount of sugar made my teeth hurt. I couldn't stop eating.

"How's Honor?" I asked, trying to stop myself from grabbing another piece.

"She's good," Layne said with a smile. "I know it's soon,

but we've started talking about getting a house someday. Like, way, way down the road. But Honor wants us to get our finances in place. She's so practical that way."

Layne made practicality sound sexy, and I had to admit, it had its appeal.

"How very domestic," Sydney said. "I can't imagine buying a house in this economy. I'll probably rent forever."

I didn't know what I was going to do. I always thought I'd make decisions like that with a significant other, or when I'd really found a place I wanted to be. Right now I was really happy with Syd, and I didn't see any need to change that arrangement.

It would be nice to own a house. Have my own little spaces where I could organize my books and put a chair in the window for reading. Maybe I'd get a dog if I had a yard. Put up some birdfeeders.

"Like I said, it's down the road. I know we're going to fight when it comes to decoration. I have no idea what I want and Honor has a very clear idea," she said with a laugh.

"I'm guessing it doesn't involve chickens," I said.

Layne shuddered. "Absolutely zero chickens."

The house that Honor lived in before she moved in with Layne was owned by the little old lady who lived next door and apparently she had a thing for chickens. Layne had sent me pictures and it was like a horror movie set. I couldn't put my finger on why seeing so many ceramic chickens and stuffed chickens and paintings of chickens was ominous, but it was.

Now just Honor's sister Lark was living there, which was good since it was only big enough for one person, really. My apartment was small, but it had two bedrooms and zero chickens.

"We're definitely going to fight about decor," Layne said, but she was smiling. "It'll be like old times when we hated each other."

"You didn't really hate each other, though, did you?" I said.

"Yeah, it was the simmering sexual tension," Sydney said.

Layne rolled her eyes. "I don't know about that. I'm just glad we got through it. But enough about me, what's the Ezra news?"

They asked me this at least three times a day and I was getting tired of having nothing much to report.

"She's doing her vanishing act again," I said. "I can't even be mad at her because she doesn't owe me anything. We're not friends, we're not dating, I have no claim on her time, except for the wedding stuff. So she's absolutely free to do whatever the hell she wants."

All of that was true, but it still hurt. A dozen times a day I'd pick up my phone to send her something and then stop myself because I didn't want to intrude on her time or be too needy.

"I'm sorry," Layne said, rubbing my arm. "That's frustrating."

"It's not a big deal. She's just my fake wedding date," I said. Layne and Sydney shared a look.

"Shut up," I said, even though neither of them had said anything. "She's just my fake wedding date and that's it."

There was a beat of silence and I knew Sydney was dying to say something, but she didn't.

"Okay," Layne said. I knew as soon as I went to the bathroom, she and Syd were going to talk about me behind my back, as friends did.

"I'm fine," I said.

"Sure," Sydney said, nodding. "That's why you've been alternating between busy and mopey all week."

"I have not been mopey," I said. I didn't think I'd been mopey. I'd been busy, sure, but mopey?

"Well, mopey for you is still pretty positive compared to other people, but we know you better," Sydney said.

"I'm not trying to be mopey," I said.

"You're just not very good at hiding your mopes," Layne said.

"I don't think that's how the word 'mopes' works," I said.

"That's not the point," Layne said. "We just want to know if you're okay. We love you and we don't want there to be a reason for mopes."

"I'm allowed to have mopes sometimes," I said. "No one can be a ray of sunshine every single day of the week. Clouds exist."

"We know," Layne said gently.

"We're meddlers and we just know if you'd like us to meddle," Sydney said, always taking the more direct approach.

"I don't need you to meddle, thank you for the offer," I said, both touched and annoyed.

"We're here for you," Layne said. "For the sunshine and the mopes."

"That sounds like a song," Sydney said.

They both started trying to write lyrics and sang in offkey voices until I put my hands on my ears and begged them to stop.

<hr />

I WAS IGNORING my mom's calls again, even after I said I wouldn't. I just needed some space and I didn't know how to get it. On Friday during lunch I finally called her back and braced for her to ask me to come to dinner on Sunday and I wasn't going to have an excuse not to. Plans with Sydney and Layne weren't enough of a reason, and the bookstore was only open until noon on Sunday.

"Oh, Joy, finally," she said.

"Hi, Mom. Sorry, I've been working a lot of hours. Book club is coming up and I've been planning and running around to get everything." That wasn't a lie, at least.

"Oh, that sounds fun. Listen, I need you to talk to Anna," she said. I knew that tone.

"What about?" I asked, setting my sandwich down. I'd come upstairs since I hadn't had the energy to pack up a lunch this morning.

"I just don't understand this resistance to the speeches. It's tradition! I just know if she doesn't do it, she's going to regret it and I don't want her to go through that."

My parents had eloped when they'd gotten married, mostly due to my maternal grandparents not approving of her marrying my dad. I still didn't really know the details of why, but they'd eloped and Mom was still upset about it so many years later. It was understandable that she wanted her daughters to look back fondly on their weddings and get to have the event that she was denied.

"Mom," I said in my gentlest voice. "I think Anna and Robert have decided what they want and if they do end up regretting it, which I don't think they will, then that's their regret to carry." I braced myself for the impact.

Mom sighed. "I just want their day to be perfect," she said. Phew.

"I know. I know you do. But you need to let them have their wedding."

I knew I'd won when she'd sighed again. "That's what your father said."

Every now and then, Dad would tell Mom his opinion and she'd listen. Rarely, but it did happen.

"So, what's your next book club theme?" she asked, moving smoothly into the next topic. I knew that my mom did love me, in her way.

I told her about the cake I was getting and the decorations and then she asked for updates on Syd and Layne and Kendra. We talked until it was time for me to go back to work and I had to shove down my sandwich in a few bites so I wasn't still hungry when I went back downstairs.

When I came through the back of the shop and headed to the front, I was surprised to find Ezra waiting by the counter for me, chatting to Kendra.

"There you are," Kendra said. "I was telling Ezra that you'd be right back."

"Hi," I said, totally thrown by her showing up again. I thought she'd at least send me a text message or something, but I guess Ezra was a fan of popping in on me when I least expected it.

"Hello, Joy," Ezra said. "Nice to see you again, Kendra."

"I've got this," Kendra said to me pushing me away from the counter. "Just take an extra-long lunch."

I should argue, but I was so fluttery at seeing Ezra again that I couldn't find the words.

"In need of fun?" I asked Ezra and the words came out sounding a little hostile. Oops.

"Yes, actually. Fun in the form of books. I read that one you gave me," she said, walking down the shelves.

"And?" I asked, practically vibrating with the need to know if she'd liked it. Honestly, if Ezra didn't like that book, I would have been seriously questioning my taste in fake wedding dates.

Ezra stopped and turned to face me. "It's an understatement to say that I loved it."

"Really?" I said, my voice squeaking. "You really loved it?"

Ezra nodded. "It was…it was perfect."

I knew exactly what she was talking about.

"You know, if you want to read other books and discuss them with a group of very nice people, our book club meets next week," I said. "You might not have time to finish the book, but that's okay. You can still come for cake and snacks and have a good time."

"Are you inviting me to your book club, Joy?" Ezra asked.

"I guess I am. Does that sound fun?"

"Reading and discussing a book does. The stranger part, not so much," she said.

"I'll be there, and sometimes Kendra comes. Sydney and Layne and Honor are in it too. I know you don't know them, but there will be at least one friendly face." I pointed at myself. "I got a cake from the best bakery. It's chocolate with rainbow stripes of frosting."

If I couldn't bribe her with the social scene, maybe I could appeal to her appetite.

"Cake, you say?"

"The best cake in the state," I said. Ezra looked away from me and let out a breath. "Maybe I'll call Esme and get the recipe for Ezraritas."

She laughed. "We're not calling them Ezraritas."

"If I stop calling them that, will you come to book club?"

"I'll think about it. How about you give me the book just in case?"

I went and found it for her and then she followed me as I pulled a few more off the shelves that I thought she should try. Figuring out her taste was like a delicious puzzle and I couldn't wait for her to read them all and tell me what she thought.

"Having fun yet?" I asked as she looked down at the pile of books I'd added to her arms.

"I'll let you know when I finish these," she said with a laugh.

"Do you get a lot of reading time?" I asked. If Ezra was cagey about her family, she was even more cagey about her daily routine, including her job. Based on the fact that she could visit me in the middle of the day, she had to be some kind of freelancer. If I ever found out what kind, I could tell her about the co-working space for freelancers in Castleton that Paige and some of her friends rented offices at.

"My days are flexible," she said.

"No nine-to-five for you, huh?"

"I've never really fit with a job like that. I did them when I had to, but now I get to make my own schedule," she said. Okay, we were getting somewhere.

"I've done all kinds of different work, but I like the security of a schedule, I guess. If I worked for myself I'd probably just read all day, and never get anything done," I said, laughing.

"It's not easy sometimes. I definitely have about twenty things I should be doing right now," Ezra said. There it was again. That bubble feeling. Like a force field had closed around us, making our own world.

"Am I distracting you, Ezra?" I asked.

"You're very distracting, Joy," Ezra said, taking a step closer. The books were in between us and I wanted to toss them to the floor so I could press myself up against her. I didn't care if everyone else saw us. They could look away if they didn't like it.

"I should probably be sorry," I said.

Ezra shook her head slightly. "Don't be."

Someone cleared their throat behind us, and I turned my head to find Kendra with an apologetic look on her face. "I am so sorry, but someone got sick in the bathroom and there's a line at the register."

Of course. I was at work, and I should be working, not doing whatever this little dance was with Ezra.

"I'll be right there," I said, looking back at Ezra. "Duty calls."

"I should probably get back to my twenty things anyway."

I wanted to ask her what kinds of things, but I had to get behind the counter and Ezra got in the line.

I got through the other sales mostly by autopilot and then she was the last person in line until three more people stepped behind her.

Damn.

"You know you can text me," I said as I slid another bookmark in between the pages of the book club book. I'd scribbled down the meeting date and time on it so she wouldn't forget, and she could show up if she wanted to.

"Maybe I will," Ezra said, taking her stack of books. "Have a good weekend, Joy."

"You too, Ezra," I said.

She slipped through the door and I went back to smiling my Customer Service smile and wondering when I was going to see her again.

∽

FIGURING EZRA WOULD VANISH AGAIN, I was surprised to get a message from her that evening as I hung out with Sydney. It was raining outside, so we'd both decided to spend the night reading on the couch. She'd gone and picked up pizza from Nick's, half pepperoni, half mushroom and pepper.

I picked up a slice of the latter and folded it in half as my phone went off.

"Huh," I said as I opened the message to read it.

"What?" Sydney said, her mouth full.

Thought you'd like to see my meager library Ezra sent with a picture of a stack of books on what looked like a windowsill. I zoomed in on the picture to see if I could figure out anything else about her house, but there wasn't much.

"Ezra just texted me a picture of the books I picked out for her," I said, typing out a response.

I guess I should show you mine since you've showed me yours I sent even though Ezra had already been to my apartment and seen the bookshelf in the living room that Sydney and I shared. I had another in my bedroom that she hadn't seen, and it was stacked two books deep. Then there were the books that I had in what were supposed to be sweater boxes under the bed. I got up and took some quick pictures and sent those back to her. It took me a couple tries to get the angle right so she didn't see the mess in my room. This weekend I needed to clean and organize and put things away.

I like the size of your…shelves Ezra sent, and I almost wanted to show Sydney the message and ask if she was flirting with me because it kind of felt like she was flirting with me.

"I'm going to eat all this pizza if you don't stop me," Sydney called, and I went back out to the living room.

"Don't you dare," I said. "You don't even like pepper and mushroom."

"Pizza is pizza," she said. "I'll make an exception."

I went back to pile my plate with as much pizza as I could so Sydney couldn't take it away from me and growled at her.

"I was just joking," she said. "I know you'd stab me in my sleep if I ate all your pizza."

"I wouldn't do something so pedestrian as stabbing," I said. "I'd have something better in mind."

Sydney narrowed her eyes. "I'm keeping my eyes on you, Joy Greene."

"Me?" I said, making my eyes big and wide. "I would never do anything wrong. Everybody loves me."

"And that's why you'd get away with it," Sydney said, taking another bite of pizza.

I finally picked up my slice and even though it had cooled, Syd was right that pizza was pizza and it was still delicious.

Since we were spending our night reading, I turned off the notifications on my phone and Ezra did stop messaging me, but that didn't stop me from checking my phone every few pages, and I had to keep switching books because I couldn't keep track of the storylines.

I was behind on my reading for work, which wasn't really

required, but which made me a better bookseller. I was always online looking up what people were talking about, hitting the industry sites to see what was coming out, and reading review blogs to see what reviewers were looking forward to. When I'd first started at the store, Kendra, Erin, and I had been kind of in the dark about what the community would want to read. Over time, we'd homed in on what titles people consistently asked for, and what books we couldn't keep on the shelves because they were so popular.

Kendra was also good friends with the librarian and got recommendations from her. Sometimes I even asked Riley and Zoey what the kids were into in terms of comics and manga, because they'd gotten totally obsessed this summer and were blazing through them.

I finally gave up on Ezra and forced myself to pay attention to my book, and that was when another message came through.

Fun? She sent with a picture of the sign at the apple orchard just outside town. I hadn't been there in ages. When I was younger, my whole family would go and hit the haunted hayride up in Redfield, but they orchard had stopped doing them years ago because it was a pain in the ass to organize and they hadn't made enough money.

Definitely fun I replied.

Tomorrow? She asked.

What time? I sent back.

I'll pick you up at two? She responded and my heart did a little flip.

"You're smiling pretty big over there," Sydney said, not looking up from her book. There was a stack of cozy mysteries beside her. I was a speedy reader, but nothing like Sydney. She could also read and walk at the same time without injuring herself. I was not so lucky on that front.

"Ezra's taking me apple picking tomorrow," I said.

"Over at the McClean Orchard?" Syd asked, turning a page.

"Yeah. She's picking me up at two. Do you want me to get you some apples or cider?"

Syd nodded. "Check and see if Layne wants some. Maybe if we bring her some apples she'll bake us a pie."

That was a good plan.

I sent a message to Layne asking about the apples and she responded right away asking if I could get her some Mackintosh and some Cortland apples and a jug of cider.

"Oh, if they have apple cider donuts and you don't bring me some, I will move your shit onto the street when you're not home and change the locks," Sydney said.

"Noted," I said, adding that to my list. I also probably should have called my mom and asked her, but I had had enough contact with her this week already.

My eyes scanned the pages of my book, but I didn't absorb any of the information. I was too busy trying to figure out what I was going to wear, and what questions to ask Ezra tomorrow. Definitely wanted to find out more about this freelance job of hers. I'd already come up with dozens of theories, each wilder than the rest. It was probably something very unexciting, like Kendra's friend Hayden, who had her own accounting business. To be fair, she did have her own side-business where she sold tie-dye shirts and scrunchies and other fun things.

Something told me Ezra wasn't an accountant. She just didn't give me accountant vibes.

I definitely considered that Ezra's job might be something that she thought wasn't socially acceptable. If it was sex work, in some form, that didn't bother me or make me think less of her. If it was something she had a passion for, then who was I to judge? It was better to do something that gave her control over her time and money and body than to let the capitalism machine grind her up and spit her out for minimum wage, which didn't even cover minimum expenses anymore.

It made me think of the writer, Skylar Alyssa, whose real name was Alessi, and she was another member of the Castleton Crew, as Kendra told me they were called. We'd done a few signings with Alessi and she'd told me that when she first started writing romance, she'd chosen a pen name out of fear that people would find out that she wrote "dirty" books. She'd worked as a school librarian at the time and had worried about being fired. It wasn't until she made enough money to quit her job that she revealed her writer identity and was willing to appear in public.

Ezra was still an enigma, and I had until my sister's wedding to figure her out.

∽

"CUTE?" I asked Sydney as I did a turn. I wore what I hoped was a casual fall look with black yoga pants tucked into my brown boots and a white long-sleeved shirt with a loose flannel vest.

"Very cute," Sydney said. She drained the rest of her coffee and did a quick check in the mirror before asking me how she looked.

Syd's shirt said "what the fucculent?" with cartoons of succulents with faces on them dancing across it paired with jeans and a beat-up pair of boots.

"Not cute," I said. "But still good." She grabbed her fall jacket and put it on.

"Where are you headed?" I asked.

"Not all of us have dates to the apple orchard. Some of us have other plans."

"What other plans?" I wasn't aware of any plans, and Sydney usually told me everything.

"Oh, just seeing where the wind blows me," she said, adjusting her boobs in the mirror.

"I'm guessing the wind is going to blow you toward an attractive woman," I said.

Sydney held up her hand and crossed her fingers. "Here's hoping."

I shook my head just as Ezra knocked on the door.

Chapter Nine

"You look just right for apple picking," Ezra said as we got in the car.

"Thanks," I said. "You look just right too."

Ezra's flannel vibe was absolutely orchard appropriate.

"I know it's probably a little childish to visit an orchard, but I don't know if I've ever been to one before. Maybe on a school trip years and years ago," Ezra said.

"What? You're from New England and you've never been to an orchard? Well, you are in for an experience, Ezra Evans," I said as she turned away from Main Street and headed in the direction of the orchard, led by the disembodied voice of the GPS in her phone.

"I'm assuming there will be apples," she said.

"There will be all kinds of apples. Cider and candy apples and caramel apples," I said.

"I don't know if I'm prepared for this apple overload," she said.

"I haven't even told you about the best part," I said. I hadn't mentioned the apple cider donuts. If you timed your visit to the little shop and café, you could get them so fresh they'd burn your fingers. Something told me that Ezra would be a fan.

"Now I'm scared," Ezra said.

"It's a good surprise, I promise," I said.

"I'm going to hold you to that."

~

WE ARRIVED and we definitely weren't the only people who had a visit to the orchard in mind for Saturday afternoon. Vans and SUVs full of adults and kids crowded the parking lot, and there were even a few dogs on leashes who were excited to get in on the fun.

Ezra parked and we got out to head with the rest of the crowd to the orchard store and café to get our picking supplies. To gain more customers, the orchard also had a service called a "personal picker" where an employee would accompany you to the orchard, do the picking, carry the apples, and let you know various apple facts.

"Would you like to have a personal picker, or let me make up apple facts that may or may not be true?" I asked.

Ezra grinned at me. "Definitely the second option. I'm happy to carry the apples."

We rented a long stick with a little cage on the end of it called a fruit picker, and a canvas bag with a drawstring at the bottom that you could undo to easily dump out the apples. Ezra started to put it on her back, but I showed her that it actually went on her front.

"This better be fun," she said as she looked down at the bag.

"Come on," I said, carrying the fruit picker and heading down an orderly row of trees.

"You may not know this, but all of these trees were planted

by hand by Johnny Appleseed back in the eighteen hundreds," I said, gesturing at the trees.

"I'm going to guess that's one of your made-up facts, Joy," Ezra said, trying to adjust the bag. I stopped walking and helped her with the straps so the bag didn't bang against her knees when she walked.

"Maybe it's true and maybe it's not," I said, wiggling my eyebrows.

We passed a mother pulling an apple out of her child's hands and tossing it on the ground. "No, that's yucky. We don't touch those ones."

"That is a true fact," I said to Ezra as we passed the now sobbing child. "Don't pick the drops. Only take directly from the tree."

"Got it," Ezra said. "None of those nasty ground apples."

I scanned the labels in front of every tree, looking for the certain apples that were my favorites in the fall.

"Ah, Cortlands. These are good. We're gonna avoid red delicious and golden delicious. Whoever named them that was a liar," I said.

"Any apple with the name delicious in it is full of shit, noted," Ezra said, looking up at the tree.

"Okay, so are you ready?" I asked.

"Show me your technique, Joy," Ezra said.

"The apples near the top ripen first, so we're going to pick from about the middle of the tree. You have to be gentle and not force an apple that's not ready," I said, raising the picker and looking for a likely candidate. I cupped the apple with the little basket and gave a quick twist of the picker to detach the apple from the tree.

"Voilà!" I said, showing Ezra the apple.

She started clapping and I felt my face going red.

"Beautiful picking performance. Tens from all the judges," Ezra said, and if she was someone else, I might have thought she was making fun of me, but her eyes twinkled, and she had a knee-melting smile on her face.

"And now we take our friend and gently place them in the bag. If you aren't gentle with the apples, they'll bruise. That's not bad if you're going to use the apples for cider or pie, but if you want to eat them, then you've got to baby them."

I looked up and realized that Ezra was right there.

"Baby the apples," Ezra said. "Don't adult the apples. And definitely don't old the apples."

I didn't realize what she'd said, so it took a second for my brain to get it and then I let out a startled laugh.

"Never old the apples, right," I said. Ezra's hair was up in her characteristic bun and my fingers ached with wanting to pull out the hair tie and see it down around her shoulders so I could run my fingers through it.

Ezra coughed. "More apples?"

"More apples," I said, collecting myself.

I pulled some more from the tree before moving on to another and then another.

"Do you want to try?" I asked Ezra. "I can take the bag for a little while."

A family with a rolling wagon went by us and I wished I'd thought of doing that. The orchard had them to rent, but I hadn't thought we'd needed one.

"I can do it and have custody of our apple babies," she said.

I made a face. "Okay, but you can't call them apple babies. Then I'll feel like a monster eating them and cooking them."

Ezra took the picker from me. "There certainly are a lot of rules about apple picking. I feel like I should be writing them down."

She looked up at the tree and selected an apple. The one she chose turned out not to be ripe, so she moved to another and with a flick of her wrist, the apple dropped into the basket of the picker.

"Congrats on picking your apple," I said as Ezra pulled the apple out to inspect it.

"Is that what the kids are calling it now?" she said, holding up the apple. "I don't feel any different."

"Was it good for you?" I asked.

She grinned. "Perfect. I feel like I need a cigarette."

"I've probably got an old vape pen from Sydney in my bag," I said.

Ezra laughed. "No, I'm good." She did take out her phone and take a picture of the apple as she held it.

"Do you want me to take one of you in your apple-picking ensemble?" I asked.

"Why not," she said, and posed with the picker as if she was holding a fishing pole.

Ezra's apple went into the bag with its friends and we ended up just strolling up and down the rows talking about things other than apples.

"I'm surprised they let people just attack their trees with very little guidance," Ezra said. "I would have thought we'd need supervision or something."

"Every tree has a camera on it, and if they catch you hurting the trees, they send the apple bouncers after you and they toss you out on your ass," I said, doing my best to keep a straight face.

"You're so full of shit, but it's cute," Ezra said, bumping me with her shoulder and throwing me off balance. I tripped on a hole in the ground and was about to fall flat on my face when Ezra grabbed me to stop the fall.

"Thanks," I said, a little breathless.

"You're welcome," she said, looking down at me. Her eyes went up and down and focused on my mouth. I almost gasped as her fingers dug into my arm.

One moment I was gazing into her eyes and the next she was pushing me backward until I came to a stop against one of the trees. Then I did gasp.

"I think it's time we practice again," Ezra said, and I didn't process what that meant, but it didn't matter.

"Yes," I said. Yes to whatever was happening right now. Yes to more. Yes to her.

Yes, Ezra, yes.

The picker had fallen out of my hands, so they were free to reach up and yank the tie out of her hair.

Ezra pushed my shoulders against the tree, the bark scraping against my spine through my shirt as her hair tumbled down. I drove my fingers through it and pulled her down to meet my mouth.

Finally.

The moment our lips touched, she moaned as if she'd been waiting for this too. Waiting for me to do exactly what I'd done.

Ezra's hair was silky in my hands and the edges of her undercut scraped my skin.

I heard a whimpering noise as Ezra clutched me and kissed me so hard that our noses and teeth clashed as we tried to get an angle that would get us closer, closer, closer.

The bag of apples was a barrier between us and I wanted to ask her to take it off, but I didn't want to end the kiss to do that, so I'd just have to deal with it in the meantime.

Ezra's teeth grazed my lower lip and she bit down on it, almost hard enough to draw blood and I moaned as she soothed the bite, sucking my lip into her mouth, caressing it with her tongue.

The kiss slowed, became deeper and less frantic, but no less intense. As if we had all the time in the world to explore and taste and test each other.

One of Ezra's hands went to the back of my neck again,

anchoring me. She seemed to like a little bit of control, and I was happy to give it to her.

The only reason I broke the kiss was the tree digging into my back had become painful and I'd shifted to try and find a better angle. Ezra pulled back and I opened my eyes to find her right there with me, her pupils large and her lips swollen.

"You okay?" she asked, and I was satisfied to see her a little breathless.

"Yeah. The tree is interfering with our make-out session though. So is this," I pushed against the apple bag.

"This orchard is conspiring against us," she said, tucking some hair behind my ear.

I finally pushed away from the tree. "I think I might have a mark." There were definitely a few scratches on my back. Worth it.

I turned around and Ezra brushed off my back, but she said she didn't see any blood or anything.

"I'm sorry. If you were uncomfortable, you should have said something." Her hand went up and down my back over my shirt.

I turned around to face her. "Your tongue was in my mouth. I was a little preoccupied."

She snorted. "I know I'm trying to be strong and everything, but these apples are really getting heavy. These straps are not comfortable." She tried to adjust the bag of apples and I found the picker on the ground.

"Okay, I think that's enough apples for today, don't you?" I asked.

"Agreed."

We walked back up the row, not talking about the kissing, even though it hung between us like a cloud.

Once we made it back to the café, we weighed our apples and paid for them and then put them in bags that I helped Ezra carry to the car.

"There, now we've had our picking experience. Our reward is in the café," I said as Ezra shut the door of her car.

"I'm just glad I don't have to carry them anymore." She rubbed her shoulder and I almost blurted out that I could give her a massage, but I didn't.

Ezra and I wandered around the store and then went to order at the café. They had coffee and tea and hot and cold cider, sandwiches, salads, and all kinds of apple desserts.

The door to the kitchen opened and a person wearing an apron brought out a tray of the most beautiful apple cider donuts I'd ever seen.

"We'll take two of those, and then a dozen to go, two coffees and two hot ciders," I said.

"Whatever she wants," Ezra said, and I looked at her, surprised.

She handed over her card and we got our drinks and donuts and took them to a table.

"You've had apple cider donuts before, right?" I asked.

Ezra shook her head.

"This is a day full of all kinds of firsts for you," I said. "I'm honored."

I raised my donut and nodded for her to do the same. We tapped our donuts together and then both took a bite, blowing on them a little to cool them.

"Oh my god," Ezra said, sucking some air into her mouth so she didn't burn her tongue as she chewed. "This is amazing."

"I know," I said, letting the donut melt on my tongue. The dough was fluffy as a cloud and was covered in cinnamon and sugar that was now all over my fingers.

Ezra devoured her donut and then licked her fingers, and that action made me think of all the other things her tongue had recently been doing and what else she might be capable of doing with it.

I pressed my legs together under the table and hoped my face wasn't too red.

"I definitely need another one of those," she said. "You?"

"I'm good," I said, still working on my first one. Ezra got up and bought another donut and came back.

"You know, I wasn't sure about coming here, but I'm glad I did. I'm glad I came with you," she said.

"Of course. Who else would know so many incredible apple facts?" I said, wiping my hands on my napkin.

Ezra snorted and started her second donut while I sipped my cider. It was spiced perfectly. I was going to make some sangria with it the next time Layne came over to hang out.

"Most of your apple facts were completely made up, but I do appreciate the effort," she said.

"Exactly. Not everyone is a fake apple facts connoisseur."

Ezra laughed again and I could see that even though her shoulders were sore from carrying the apples, she was having a good time. This was the Ezra I'd seen in the bar.

"Did you go to the orchard a lot with your family?" she asked.

"Not a ton, but we definitely came at least once every fall. Anna wanted to have her wedding here, actually, but you would not believe how expensive it is to have a wedding in an orchard." When Anna had told me the amount, I almost fell off the couch. She and Robert had decent jobs, but they were being very practical about their wedding and would rather save for a house.

"Now it's more fun to go with my nieces and nephew, but they get tired after a really short time. It will be nice when they're older and can appreciate it more. Not that I don't adore all of them now."

"They adore you," Ezra said.

"Well, that's because I'm the fun one that slips them an extra piece of candy and lets them skip naptime," I said with a laugh. "I hope that when they're older if they get into a situation they know they can call me and I won't judge them."

Ezra sat back in her chair. "That's a good person to have in your life."

"Did you ever have someone like that?" I asked.

Ezra shook her head slowly. "No. I was pretty much on my own."

"I'm sorry," I said.

She shrugged one shoulder. "It's not your fault, Joy. It's in the past. I've moved on."

I wanted to ask her if she really had, because this whole lone-wolf thing she had going on seemed pretty connected to not trusting people, but I kept my mouth shut.

Ezra finished her donut and licked her fingers again, and this time I forced myself to look away so I didn't have all kinds of dirty thoughts at the apple orchard café with a family with three kids sitting next to us.

Ezra helped me carry all the other bags of apples to the car for my friends.

"I can't remember the last time I had an apple pie," she said as we got in the car.

"If Layne makes one, I'll save you a piece," I said. "But the only rule is that you have to come over if you want to eat it."

Ezra laughed. "It's a deal."

She drove us back to my apartment and I couldn't help but feel a sense of loss as she pulled into the parking lot.

"I'll help you bring everything upstairs," she said.

"Great, yeah, thanks," I said.

Ezra and I hauled the bags of apples and donuts and cider upstairs and I saw that Sydney was still out doing whatever it was she was doing. Or whomever. She hadn't hooked up in a while, so I was actually surprised she was getting back to her regular routine.

"I should probably get going," Ezra said. "Unless…"

I grabbed onto that one word. "Unless?"

"Unless you maybe wanted to get some dinner?"

"Yes, that sounds great!" I said immediately and then wished I could take back my enthusiasm. Oops.

I coughed a few times. "Did you want me to pick? Or were you in the mood for something?"

"You know, I've lived here for a few months now and I haven't eaten a lobster yet. Do you know where we could get one?" Ezra asked.

"Absolutely," I said. I sent Sydney a message that I was going out for dinner and if she got back she was on her own.

"Let's go," I said.

Chapter Ten

I GAVE Ezra directions instead of letting her use the GPS. We headed back to Redfield, but not to my parents' house, and ended up at one of my favorite places. Outside, it was covered in white peeling paint and didn't look that impressive, but all the best places were like that.

Ezra had to go around the parking lot twice before she found a spot just as someone was pulling out.

"This place is crowded," she said as she turned off the car.

"There's a reason for that," I said. "Come on."

We got out of the car and Ezra gave me a look that she wasn't so sure about this.

"It'll be fun. Promise," I said. "Would I lead you astray?"

Ezra narrowed her eyes.

I made my eyes wide and innocent and she cracked, laughing softly.

"Let's go get you some lobster, Ezra," I said, heading for the door.

The entryway for Red's Lobster Shack was so packed that Ezra couldn't even come all the way in, and the door rested partway open.

"Is it always like this?" Ezra asked.

"Pretty much. They're only open until Halloween, though, so you can't come here in the winter."

It took some work, but I made it to the counter and said I needed a table for two and was handed a buzzer before I pushed my way back to Ezra, the buzzer clutched in my hand.

"Success," I said as I showed her the buzzer.

"How long do you think it's going to be?" Ezra said, looking around at the crowd.

"She said fifteen minutes or so," I said. "They're very efficient here."

Ezra seemed doubtful, but some space opened up so she could move away from the door and lean against the wall, her arms crossed.

"This place is an institution," I said. "I'm surprised you haven't heard of it before. It's been on a bunch of travel shows and cooking shows. In the height of the summer the line is all the way out the door and into the parking lot. Sometimes it even goes down the street."

Ezra shuddered. "I'm glad that's not the case now."

"I wouldn't have brought you here. My idea of fun isn't standing in a line."

"And yet theme parks manage to draw millions of visitors each year," Ezra said.

"Well, you get a reward for waiting in line. Unlike at the DMV."

Ezra chuckled. "I guess that's right."

As people got buzzed for their tables, more people arrived, so there were about the same amount of people waiting.

"We'd only come here on special occasions when I was a kid," I said. "It was a lot of work to bring four kids to a restaurant."

"I bet," Ezra said.

Not for the first time, I wondered if Ezra was an only child.

"But Mom made us learn restaurant manners. Not like what you saw when you came over. We had to learn volume control, and that yelling at each other across the butter wasn't acceptable in public."

I knew I was trying to fill the silence, but Ezra didn't seem to mind. The bad part was that it did feel like I was only talking about myself.

"We had this diner in my hometown that I used to go to with Joel and Alex. We'd get cheese fries and milkshakes and avoid going home. There was this waitress, Janie, who used to slip us free fries. I think she felt bad for us."

"She sounds great," I said.

Ezra laughed. "She was a tough old bird. She was mean as hell to your face but then you'd realize that she gave you free ice cream. She's probably dead now. Or she looks exactly the same. I swear, some people like that are ageless."

"You should go back and see if she's still there," I said. Ezra shook her head.

"No, I don't go back there." Her eyes met mine.

"Because of your family," I guessed.

"Because of my family," she confirmed. "I know I haven't told you much of anything."

"It's okay," I said.

The buzzer went off and our conversation was interrupted by getting seated at our table. It was set for two, with one of those red and white checkered plastic tablecloths. The chairs and the table might be rickety, but the restaurant was spotless.

The server was young, but she had an air of someone who knew what she was doing. She brought us water and handed out menus and rattled off the specials with a practiced efficiency.

Ezra didn't speak to me until she'd left to handle another table.

"My family is…difficult. There's all kinds of issues and I

did whatever I could to get out and cut off all ties. I know people think that makes me selfish, but I don't care. I've been through a lot to have the life that I have now. And I'm not sorry."

She looked at me as if I was going to challenge her. To tell her that yes, that was selfish.

"I'm glad you chose yourself," I said.

It took her a while to respond.

"Thank you," she said.

"You're welcome."

She opened the menu and then closed it again. "You don't want details? Most people do."

"No. I trust you had your reasons. You wouldn't have done something so extreme as cutting contact if you didn't have a good reason," I said.

"Trust me, I did. Many reasons," she said, running her finger along the edge of the menu.

"You definitely deserve lobster, then," I said, hoping to bring things around to a lighter place.

Ezra looked up at me and while she wasn't smiling, her face was soft.

"I think so," she said.

~

IN THE END we ordered the twin lobster dinner, which came with corn, baked potatoes, rolls, and a small bucket of drawn butter.

"Are you ready?" I asked, picking up the lobster cracker.

"As I'll ever be," Ezra said.

I showed her how to dismember the lobster, which was gross if you thought about it too much, so I told her not to think about it too much.

"I hope you don't care about getting that shirt messy. No

matter how hard you try to stay clean, it's a losing battle. Lobster is a messy food." It also wasn't a very sexy food, but I didn't say that.

Ezra dipped a bit of claw meat into the butter and popped it into her mouth.

"You're right, this was totally worth it," she said.

The corn was still sweet and the rolls were fresh-baked and fluffy inside.

"You're getting all the best of Maine today, between the lobster and the apple cider donuts," I said as she attacked the lobster, trying to get the most out of it.

"I'm not complaining," she said, digging around one of the claw knuckles to see if anything was left. The food was delicious, but even more enjoyable was watching Ezra enjoy herself. She savored everything and wasn't shy about asking for more butter when we ran out. She methodically ate every single thing, and even finished my potato for me.

I passed her wet wipes and we cleaned ourselves off, sitting back in the plastic chairs.

"Holy shit," she said. "I feel like that was some sort of challenge I just won."

I laughed. "We'll get you a little lobster trophy. I wonder what the record is for most lobsters eaten in one sitting?"

"I don't want to know," she said.

Our server came back and asked us if we wanted dessert. Ezra's eyes gleamed.

"Split something?" she asked.

"I do have a craving for a peanut butter whoopie pie," I said. I'd seen them on the menu.

"We'll take that and two forks," Ezra said to the server.

"You don't eat a whoopie pie with a fork," I said. "Have you never had one of those either?"

"Maybe? What do they look like?"

For someone who was born and raised in New England, she really was lacking in a lot of experiences.

The whoopie pie arrived on a plate and the server gave us two forks without comment. I used the fork to divide the whoopie pie into halves and pushed one at Ezra.

"I've had one of these before, I think," she said, picking up her half.

"You haven't had these ones and they're the best." They were just about as good as the ones they had at Sweet's, but I was never going to admit that to anyone in Arrowbridge or Castleton, or risk bodily harm.

"Mmm," Ezra said, closing her eyes. The way she enjoyed food was almost sexual and it gave me warm feelings below the waist.

I could barely concentrate on my whoopie pie half as I watched Ezra devour hers. Had it only been a few hours ago that she'd been pushing me up against an apple tree and biting my lower lip?

Now I couldn't think about anything else.

Ezra finished her dessert and the server brought the check. She grabbed it before I could even try to reach for it.

"I told you. I'm footing the fun bill," she said, pulling her card out of her wallet.

"Fine," I said. "But I'd like it noted that I did try to pay."

Ezra handed the check off to the server as she passed.

"So, I have to know, on a scale of one to ten, how much fun did you have today?" I asked. "If you say one, then we've got a problem."

"Hmmm, I'd have to think about that. The apple orchard was definitely a solid eight. Lobster was a nine, and this whoopie pie was a ten. So that would make the whole day a nine on average."

I rolled my eyes. "You're just being nice. Come on, what did you really think?"

Ezra leaned forward and said, "I think I'd like to take you to the bathroom and practice kissing you, but I wasn't going to say that out loud."

Oh.

She sat back with a smirk on her face. "How's that for a rating?"

I opened my mouth and then closed it. What were we doing? This was all fake, right? Ezra was just messing with me. Trying to get a rise out of me.

Sure, she'd kissed me in the apple orchard, but that was… just messing around.

"So why did you say it out loud?" I asked.

Ezra's eyes stared into mine. "Why do you think, Joy?"

"I can't read your mind, Ezra. I have no idea what you're thinking at any given moment. You're a complete fucking mystery."

I couldn't help myself as I started shredding my napkin.

She opened her mouth to say something and then closed it, looking away from me.

"We should get going."

~

THE RIDE back to my apartment was silent, and not in a good way. There was companionable silence, and then there was thick, awkward silence that you could taste in the air.

This was definitely the second, and I didn't like it.

"Thanks for dinner," I said, even though it felt like a silly thing to say.

"You're welcome," Ezra said. She didn't seem to want to look directly at me.

"And, um, let me know about book club. You should come," I said.

"I'll think about it," Ezra said.

"And then we have the bridal shower on Saturday," I said, and I felt like a nag, but I just couldn't take the quiet.

"Right," Ezra said, nodding.

"Are you mad at me or something?" I asked. "If you are, you can just tell me instead of being a silent weirdo."

I guess my fuse was shorter than normal. Usually I would have just let it go and waited until she decided she wanted to talk again, but maybe the lobster had given me courage or something.

That made Ezra look at me finally.

"Just go inside, Joy," she said with a heavy sigh. "Just go inside."

"Why? What's wrong with you? Why are you suddenly so eager to get rid of me?"

Back at the restaurant she'd been pretty much saying the opposite.

"Joy…" she said, a warning tone in her voice. "I shouldn't have said anything, let's just forget it."

"Said what, Ezra?"

"Can we just drop this?" Her hands gripped the steering wheel and I could tell this was getting to her. Fine. She shouldn't say things like that if she didn't want me to react to them.

"You're impossible, you know that? Fine, you want to drop it, fine. Goodnight." I got out of the car before she could say anything.

I knew, to her, it probably looked like I was storming away in a huff, but really, I was backing down from a fight. I'd always been the first one to cave in an argument, even if I was right. At least this time I'd gotten to add a dramatic flounce instead of like, crying and apologizing at the same time. That was always so embarrassing.

I stomped upstairs and shut the apartment door a little too hard.

"Whoa, what happened?"

I wasn't expecting Sydney to be home until tomorrow. She usually spent the night with her hookups and then escaped the next morning before they woke up.

"Nothing," I said. I checked my phone, wondering if Ezra was going to text, but she didn't. Fine. That was just fine.

"Joy?" Sydney asked, coming over to me. I had my back against the front door and my fists clenched.

"Nothing. It's nothing. I just had a fight with Ezra. I think. I don't know. It's all very confusing, Syd."

I was struck by a wave of exhaustion so intense that I almost slid to the floor in a heap.

"Aw, sweetheart," Syd said, putting her arm around me and leading me to the couch before she went to make some tea.

"I don't want to talk about it," I called to her as she moved around the kitchen.

"Then you don't have to talk about it," she said. "We can talk about something else."

That sounded much better to me. I'd rather escape my own drama for a little bit.

"Do you want to hear about my terrible date?" she asked.

I propped myself on the back of the couch so I could see her. "You know I do."

"Okay, so you know I've been on kind of a hookup hiatus, so to speak," she said.

"Uh huh," I said as she got out two mugs.

"Well anyway, I decided I really needed to have sex, so I jumped back on my apps and decided to have a little fun today. Anyway, found this girl who lives twenty minutes away that's up for a hookup, so I figure, great. Sounds good. Afternoon delight."

I made a face and she laughed. The kettle went off and she made up each cup before continuing her story.

"So, you know, I'm into safety so I get her to agree to meet at a restaurant near her place, in case I get the green light. Firstly, she picks this really tacky chain place, but you know what, I'm not picky. Whatever."

Sydney continued and I followed along on her terrible date as the girl proceeded to show up with her husband in tow. They'd been looking for a third and Sydney was absolutely not into that.

"I mean, it's false advertising! Stop trying to be shady! I'm not into it. Been there, tried that, did not want the T-shirt. So anyway, I'm sitting with these two fuckers and it's happy hour. I figure I might as well get a drink and some appetizers for my trouble."

"And?" I asked.

"Those mother fuckers ordered a bunch of food, stuffed their faces, and then ditched me with the bill. I thought it was weird that they both disappeared to the bathroom at the same time, but I figured they were just banging or something. Huge fucking scam. I'm so pissed."

Sydney sat back on the couch and ran her hand through her hair.

"So your date, or whatever that was, can't have been worse than me having to fork out money for two assholes."

No. In my case, the asshole had paid, and I wasn't even sure if she was even being an asshole.

My anger and frustration at Ezra had cooled a little bit, and now I was ready to see what Sydney thought.

I explained the day we'd spent, the kiss, then the dinner and Ezra's comment, my response, and then her silent treatment.

"And now I'm just really confused. I'm pretty sure she was just fucking with me, and was mad that I called her on it, but I just…she doesn't make any sense!"

Sydney sat for a second and looked at me, then took one of my hands in hers. "I'm going to say something that I've said before, but I really need you to hear me: Ezra. Wants. To. Fuck. You." She enunciated each word and squeezed my hand for emphasis.

"She has a weird way of telling me, if that's true," I said.

"Joy. My love. She literally said she wanted to take you to the bathroom. How much clearer could she have been?"

I opened my mouth to argue and then slammed it shut.

"But she's always saying kind of flirty stuff like that. It doesn't mean anything."

"Did you, or did you not, make out with this exact same woman in an apple orchard today?"

I nodded.

"I don't know about you, but I don't usually make out with people that I'm not attracted to. At least not when I'm sober."

"Okay, say that she is attracted to me. It's not serious. We don't want the same things. If I know one thing about Ezra it's that she is good on her own and she's not into any kind of commitment. And that's what I want. I want it all. I want love, I want someone who's committed to me. Who's willing to risk it all for a chance at love."

Sydney smiled. "There's my romantic girl. If that's what you want, you should have it. Tell Ezra. I know you're not good at the whole confrontation thing, but you've got to make it clear what you want and that if she can't give it to you, then you need to just be friends, or cut things off now."

That seemed like a reasonable suggestion, but I felt nauseated at the idea of telling that to Ezra.

"You're right, I know you're right. I need to talk to her. Sooner rather than later."

I cringed and Syd squeezed my shoulder. "I'm here for support, or if you want to practice."

"Thanks," I said. "I'm sorry about your terrible date. I feel like we should go out and have dinner tomorrow to make up for it."

"Deal," Syd said, scooting over so she could put her head on my shoulder.

"What would you do without me?" she said.

"I have no idea," I said with a laugh.

∼

I COULDN'T SLEEP that night, thinking about all this shit with Ezra. I even checked my phone a few times to see if she'd sent any messages, but nothing.

The next day I even expected that I'd get a message from her saying that she wasn't going to be my wedding date after all.

"I think you're going to have to reach out first," Sydney said. "Let me know if you want me to type out the message for you." Syd had done that for me before, and even sent messages to my mom or sisters when I'd been too scared.

"I'm going to wait a day," I said, "just in case she comes to her senses."

"Okay, but I'm going to bug you about this until you do it," she said, narrowing her eyes. "Layne and Honor asked if they could come to dinner with us, on another subject."

"Of course they can, they don't have to ask."

Ever since we'd added Honor via Layne to our group, I think she felt awkward about assuming that she was included.

"That's what I said. Cool. Honor heard about this new place in Hartford that she wants to try. I'm sending you the menu."

My phone buzzed with the message from Sydney. Neither of us ever went to a restaurant without checking out the menu first.

I scanned through quickly and saw they had burgers and steaks and typical American cuisine. Not too fancy, but just a tiny bit upscale.

"Ohhh, that burger with the bacon fig jam sounds good," I said.

"I know, that's exactly what I was looking at," Syd said. "Honor wants to make a reservation, so I'll tell her we're good."

"Works for me," I said.

I spent the rest of the day definitely not thinking about Ezra. Not thinking about her while Syd made pancakes. While I did a few loads of overdue laundry. While I checked my bank account. While I cleaned out my car. While I made sandwiches for lunch.

"Joy," Sydney said, snapping her fingers in front of my face. "I've been talking to you and you're completely checked out. You've got to talk to Ezra. Not tomorrow. Today." She handed me my phone.

"Be brave," she said.

I'd said the same thing to Ezra about reading the books I'd recommended.

"Ugh, okay," I said, pulling up a new message to Ezra. It took me a few minutes to craft a text and I read it aloud to Syd.

"How's this? Hi Ezra, I think we really need to sit down and talk about what's going on between us and figure out how to move forward. When is a good time for you to meet?"

Syd digested the message. "Sounds very professional, which is good, since there is money involved. Go ahead and send."

With the approval from Syd, I went ahead and sent the message and immediately turned my notifications off so I wouldn't be stressing about her response for the rest of the day. That had been another suggestion from Syd. She'd even threatened to take my phone from me.

"I know we're going to dinner in a little bit, but I think we need to get out a little bit first," Syd said. "Get your jacket and come on."

She fed Clementine and then we just wandered around

Arrowbridge, heading down residential streets and waving to people passing by as they walked their dogs, or pulled their children in wagons. We knew pretty much everyone, so sometimes we'd have to stop and chat and say hello to a dog, or I'd ask how a kid liked a book I'd picked out for them. To be fair, it was less of a walk and more of a stroll with a lot of chatting.

I took a quick shower when we got back and purposely did not check my phone, continuing my Ezra-free evening.

Honor volunteered to drive, so she picked both of us up and we piled into the backseat of her fancy car with the leather seats. Honor hadn't grown up with money, but Mark paid well and she'd been frugal.

Layne asked for an Ezra update and I told her what had happened last night.

"So I sent her a text asking if we could talk and then I haven't checked my phone," I said.

"I'm very proud," Sydney said.

Layne looked back at me from the front seat. "I am too, good for you, Joy. Don't put up with bullshit."

"Agreed," Honor chimed in from the driver's seat.

We reached the restaurant and it was good we'd gotten a reservation, because it was packed. I couldn't help but flash back to my lobster dinner last night with Ezra and everything that had gone down.

A server seated us in a cushy booth and handed us menus that were so new they didn't even have any streaks or stains on them. I listened politely to the specials, but I'd already decided what I wanted earlier when I'd looked at the menu.

"Drinks?" Layne asked.

"Yes," I said.

"Same," Sydney said. She hadn't told her awful date story yet, but I knew Layne was going to love it.

Honor abstained since she was driving, but she didn't seem to mind.

Sydney and I ordered the bacon jam burger, Layne got fried chicken, and Honor got the sirloin.

Once Sydney had finished her first drink and ordered her second, she recounted the date story and even though I'd already heard it, I still laughed.

Honor rolled her eyes. "People are disgusting."

"They're the worst," Layne said. "This is why I avoided online dating."

"Now you don't have to worry about it," Honor said and shared a soft look with Layne.

"Thank goodness."

We'd ordered some appetizers and started sharing stories of awful dates. Honor had some good ones about rich men she'd dated in her attempt to marry for money before she'd met Layne. I would have thought Layne didn't want to hear those kinds of things, but she cackled and laughed the whole time.

"Aren't you glad that I saved you from marrying rich?" Layne said, wrinkling her nose at Honor.

"Most days," Honor said, but her eyes twinkled with the joke. Layne pretended to be offended until she leaned in and kissed Honor.

The dinner was fun, but in the back of my mind I couldn't stop wondering if Ezra had responded. If she would ever respond. It could happen that she could completely ghost me.

Since dinner wasn't complete without dessert, we ordered four and shared them with each other, swapping plates and stealing bites.

"Oh, I'm so full, that burger was amazing," Sydney said, both hands on her stomach as Honor drove us back.

"I know. I'm going to see if I can figure out how to make bacon fig jam. It can't be that hard," Layne said, pulling out her phone and muttering to herself.

"I hope you're ready to have a house full of jam," Sydney said to Honor.

"I think I'll find some way to manage," she said. "I'll just have to make a lot of charcuterie boards."

"Listen, if you need any help with getting rid of any extra charcuterie you may have, I volunteer," Sydney said.

"Me too," I agreed.

Honor laughed and I was pleased to hear that sound. She laughed a lot with Layne, but it took her some time to warm up to other people.

Thinking about Honor taking time to trust people made me circle right back around to Ezra. So many of my thoughts seemed to meander right back to her.

I pulled out my phone and Sydney snatched it out of my hand.

"Absolutely not. You're not checking anything until we get home," she said, holding my phone up.

"Hey!" I said, reaching for it.

"Now, children, you behave back there. Honor will pull this car over," Layne said, using her stern voice that she'd honed in her nanny job.

"Give me my phone," I said to Syd. She was being ridiculous.

"Only if you agree to not check anything until we're home."

"What difference does it make?" I said and she rolled her eyes and handed the phone back.

"Fine. Be that way," she said.

I checked my messages and my heart jumped as I saw a new message from Ezra.

I'm free Monday night. Where did you want to meet?

Both hands shook a little as I tried to figure out how to respond. Did I want to do this in public? Not really. In case things got intense, I didn't want other people seeing that. No, it was better to do this at my apartment. Plus, it was more comfortable, and I could kick her out and lock the door if I wanted to. I didn't foresee a situation that would require that, but you never knew.

"Hey, so Ezra is going to come over tomorrow to talk, but can you stay with me, just in your room? Just in case?" Syd was going to be my backup parachute. Plus, it would be good to have her there for after.

"Of course. I promise not to eavesdrop too much," she said.

"Do you need me too? I'm happy to be there," Layne said.

"No, I think I'll be okay." It would be nice to have Layne, but I didn't want to beg her and feel like a baby who couldn't have a grown-up conversation without her besties to back her up.

"You've got this," Layne said. "Maybe I'll bring you a piece of pie after."

"You're not giving away all our pie," Honor said.

"That's what she said," Sydney said, loud enough for everyone to hear. I snorted and Layne laughed, and Honor scowled in the rearview mirror.

"There's enough of my pie for everyone to enjoy it," Layne said, and Honor let out a laugh.

"Pie would be great," I said, and everyone was silent. "Not like that!"

They all laughed at me.

Chapter Eleven

Monday was a slow day at work, and I couldn't find enough tasks to keep my mind occupied as I waited for closing time so I could go up and clean the apartment before Ezra showed up.

At last it was time to lock up the shop and I dashed upstairs, beating Sydney. I chucked some kibble in Clementine's bowl and did a mad dash around to put things away and wipe down counters and arrange the pillows on the couch.

Sydney arrived right in the middle of my cleaning frenzy, and she put both hands on my shoulders. "I love you, but you need to calm down."

"I know," I said. I couldn't explain why I was creating a mountain out of this. Why did it matter so much?

Syd was still giving me a pep talk when there was a knock at the door.

"Shit, that's her," I said, smoothing my hands over my hair.

"I'm going to be in my room trying to mind my own business. If you need anything, just yell 'candy nipples!' and I'll come running."

"Candy nipples?" I asked as Ezra knocked again.

"Not something you'd say in regular conversation, is it?" Syd called as she shut herself in her room.

I mean, she had a point. Unless you were inside some kind of erotic sweets store, you probably wouldn't be talking about candy nipples.

I opened the door and there was Ezra, her face as inscrutable as ever.

"Hey," I said, "come in."

She came in and let Clementine do his inspection and then pulled off her shoes before following me to the couch.

"So," Ezra said. "What did you want to talk about?"

I really wished I was covered in a blanket for comfort, but that seemed juvenile, so I just sat there with my hands in my lap.

"What are we doing?" I asked. "What is this?" I gestured between us. "Are you serious about wanting to be with me, or is it just a casual thing for you, or what? Because I don't do casual relationships, Ezra."

I looked up from my lap and into her eyes. "If all you want is something casual, then this isn't going to work out. If you were just play flirting and weren't serious, then whatever, but I need to know. You have to talk to me, Ezra."

My body shook a little as I took a deep breath. There. That hadn't been that bad.

Ezra looked away from me and out the window and then back. She swallowed and I watched her throat. It was a very sexy throat. Even now, I wanted to lean over and lick her skin, and maybe even leave a mark.

"I don't know what we are, Joy. I seriously don't." She dragged her hand across her face and for the first time since she walked in, I noticed how pale she was and that there were circles under her eyes, as if she hadn't slept.

"I didn't intend for this to be anything. When I first saw you and you said you wanted me to be your wedding date, I thought it would just be a fun thing to do with a cute girl. A story that I'd look back on of something impulsive I did when I was younger. You seemed to want to keep things professional and you were so sweet that I suggested the money to try and put up a barrier, I don't know."

She sighed again and pulled the pillow from behind her back into her lap, holding onto it like an anchor.

"I don't do this, Joy. I don't do relationships, I don't do connections, I don't do emotions. Well, I try not to do emotions, but sometimes they get the best of me. But then I kept wanting to spend time with you and I couldn't get enough. You're adorable and funny and you love your friends and you're just like this warm light and I wanted to be around you. I kept telling myself it was just for practice or whatever bullshit, but really it was just you. It was just you, Joy."

Our eyes met and my body temperature rose a few degrees. I wasn't used to hearing such nice things said to me by someone so beautiful.

"It's so fucking frustrating, you have no idea. Every time I'd leave, I'd have this pep talk with myself and I'd say I was going to stay away from you, get you out of my system, but then I'd email you or text you or show up at the bookstore, just because I wanted to see your reaction. See what you'd say. I don't get this way, Joy, and it's freaking me the fuck out." Her voice had gotten progressively louder and she'd started gesturing with her hands. This was a side of Ezra I'd never seen, but it was doing things to me.

"I'm not sure how to respond to that," I said slowly.

"You don't have to say anything, Joy. This is my fuck up. I'll deal with it. I'll get over it."

Hold up.

"Wait, what?" I asked. "Why do you need to get over it?"

Ezra blinked at me. "Because you don't feel the same way.

And I don't think you want to take a crash-relationship course with me. I'm a disaster, Joy. You deserve so much better."

What the fuck was she talking about?

Words had power, as a bookseller this was a fact I knew to be true. But sometimes, you needed action.

I yanked the pillow out of Ezra's hands and straddled her lap. She made a surprised sound.

"You're not a disaster," I said, before kissing her.

She hadn't expected the kiss either, but her shock was short-lived, and she kissed me back, her hands that had been on the pillow digging into my sides and pulling me closer.

This was one way to have a conversation, I thought, and smiled into her mouth.

She pulled back after a second.

"What's so funny?" she asked, pushing my hair out of the way.

"This whole situation. I really thought you were flirting with me because you were messing with me. Syd told me that you were trying to tell me how you felt, but I guess I just didn't think that could be true."

"You're amazing, Joy. And I'd be a giant asshole to treat you that way. I was attracted to you from the beginning and I thought it would go away. It just got stronger and now I don't have any fucking clue what happens next."

I looked down at her and brushed my thumb along her bottom lip.

"I have a few ideas of what we can do. And as far as the rest of it, we'll figure it out. See where this goes. I think we owe it to ourselves to at least give it a shot."

Ezra licked my thumb and nodded slowly. "I think I can try that."

I chuckled. "Don't sound so enthusiastic."

Ezra closed her eyes. "The physical part doesn't scare me.

It's the rest of it. I don't...I can't trust people. I don't trust people."

She opened them and looked up at me and I'd never seen someone so completely vulnerable before. Just being here with me like this, admitting these things was a huge act of trust.

"I know," I said. "And I can't promise this won't turn into a complete mess, but if we don't try, we won't know."

This was also going to be scary for me. I hadn't been in a committed relationship in a while. I didn't get into committed relationships unless I was really, really sure about someone.

I wasn't sure about Ezra. She was still too much of a wild card.

"Just promise you won't just ghost me. If you decide that you don't want to be with me, just tell me. It'll hurt way less than if you just stop communicating. Okay?"

Ezra nodded. "I promise not to ghost you. Even though it goes against a lot of my natural instincts."

"I know," I said ruefully. "I'm learning this about you. I'll just start calling you Lone Wolf."

Ezra snorted. "That's not the worst nickname I've ever had, but I'm not a fan."

"I like your name. It's a good one," I said.

"Thanks. I'm not responsible for it, but it's the one thing my parents seemed to get right, so I guess I should be grateful for that," she said.

"Will you tell me more about your life? Not the bad stuff, but the good stuff. I feel like when we're together I'm always talking about me." I laughed.

"I like talking about you better," Ezra said, her hands sliding up and down my sides, distracting me. Every pass she made lifted my sweater a little bit higher.

"I know, but this can't be one-sided. That's my other requirement. That you talk to me about stuff. Don't go silent for days on end. If you need to take a break, that's cool. Just say 'hey, need to go off the grid and take some time, I'll let you know when I'm good.'"

"I can do that," Ezra said. "It's going to be an adjustment, thinking about someone else. You'll have to be patient with me."

"I can do *that*," I said.

Ezra's fingers drifted into my hair, pulling my face down toward hers. "Now that we got the guidelines taken care of, can we do something else?" she said, her breath sliding across my skin.

"What did you have in mind?" I said, already breathless even though she hadn't kissed me yet.

"Oh, I have some ideas," she said, but just before our lips met, there was a loud noise that startled both of us.

"Candy nipples! Candy nipples!" Sydney yelled and Ezra held onto me so I didn't fall off the couch.

"Jesus Christ, Syd, what the hell?"

Sydney didn't look that apologetic. "Sorry. I just really have to pee."

"You could have just said, 'excuse me'," I said, hoping Ezra wasn't too annoyed.

"I mean, I could have, but you two looked pretty cozy so I figured the only way to get your attention was by yelling something." When she said it that way, it sounded so reasonable.

"Why 'candy nipples'?" Ezra asked, turning her head to the side.

"Because it's not something you'd bring up in casual conversation."

"You have a safe word?" Ezra said, looking at me.

"Not exactly," I said, glaring at Sydney who just smirked at me.

"I think I'm missing something," Ezra said.

"It's okay, I'll explain later." After I murdered my roommate.

"Okay, well, as you were," Syd said, gesturing at us before heading to the bathroom.

The door closed, but we could still hear her loudly humming to herself.

"I'm sorry," I said, ducking my head and hiding my face in Ezra's neck.

"Hey, no big deal," Ezra said. "I've met Sydney before. I think she was just worried about you, in her way."

I snorted and raised my head. "Why don't we, um, go have some privacy?"

Going to my room was taking things up a notch, and I hoped Ezra didn't think I was suggesting that we should just fall into bed immediately.

Ezra agreed and I got up off her and took her hand as we went into my room and shut the door.

I sat on the bed and let Ezra roam around the small space, taking everything in.

"It's cozy," she said, looking over at me as she scanned my bookshelves, pulling out some of the first line of books so she could see the volumes stacked behind.

"Are they arranged in any special way?"

"Yes, but only in a way that I understand. If I tried to explain it to anyone else, it wouldn't make sense." I'd created my own filing system based on my needs, and what I was currently reading. I liked keeping track of what I'd read visually, as well as with my tracking spreadsheet. I took reading very seriously.

"Then I won't mess them up," Ezra said, finally turning around to face me. It had been so easy to climb into her lap just a few moments ago, but now we were in my room. With my bed. The bed that symbolized so many possibilities. Not to mention the vibrators and lube I had in the table right next to the bed.

I tried to breathe as Ezra sat next to me on the bed.

"Scared?" she asked me.

"No," I lied.

"Come here, I have something to tell you," she said, crooking her finger at me.

"What is it?" I asked, leaning in. It seemed weird that she had to whisper something when we were the only two people in the room, but I went with it.

Ezra's breath was warm in my ear. "Candy nipples," she said.

I burst into laughter, unable to stop myself.

"Better?" she asked as I got a hold of myself.

"Yes," I said, swallowing the giggles.

"You're so cute, Joy."

People were always calling me cute. I tried not to be resentful about it.

"What else am I?" I asked, scooting back on the bed, hoping she'd take the invitation.

Ezra gave me one of those smiles that had just a little edge of danger. The smile that had made me ask her to be my wedding date in the first place.

Ezra crawled onto the bed with me, propping herself up with her arms as her body settled atop mine.

"You're sexy, and hilarious, and caring, and your smile makes me feel like I've been given a gift."

"Oh, I like that," I said. "What about the rest of me?"

Ezra stared into my face and said, "Well, your body is also good."

"Good? That's it?" I said, almost sitting up in indignation.

Ezra laughed. "Your lips in particular, are perfection. I haven't been able to stop thinking about them."

With one finger, she traced my lips and I had to stop myself from flicking my tongue out and tasting her skin.

"In fact, I think I need to do this," she said before she

replaced her finger with her mouth. I arched upward into her, trying to get closer.

Ezra's hips pressed into mine and she shifted, so that one of her legs slid between mine.

Oh. That was nice.

She explored my mouth, as if we hadn't kissed before. As if she was savoring every lick and inhale we shared between us.

My hands flew to her hips, fingers digging in so I had something to hold onto as she kissed me like she was drowning and I was her oxygen.

There was an intensity to Ezra's kiss that almost scared me. I'd never kissed someone quite like her before.

As if from their own volition, my hips started thrusting against her leg, seeking friction. Even though we were both fully clothed, I could feel the scorching heat of her body through the layers and my pussy ached for more.

Ezra moved against me as she moaned in her throat and the kiss faltered briefly as we both rubbed against each other.

"Yes," I said, before I kissed her again, holding onto her hips as they thrust against my leg and I sought my own satisfaction against hers. After a quick adjustment, I was hitting the right spot and even if I had a rash or chafing from this, I didn't give a flying fuck. Any injuries sustained while getting off with Ezra were worth it.

She pulled back and rested her forehead against mine, her face contorted with concentration so sexy that I almost came then.

"I'm close," she said.

"Me too," I gasped, moving faster and reveling in how many sounds Ezra made.

"Right there, right there," she panted, and then her hips jerked as she came, throwing her head back and letting out moans that I knew Sydney could hear through the door. I reveled in those sounds as they set off my own climax, my entire body shuddering as waves of heat and pleasure radiated through me, leaving warm tingles in their wake. At last, our bodies stopped shaking and I opened my eyes to find Ezra smiling down at me, her cheeks pink, and a slight sheen of sweat on her forehead.

"That wasn't what I came here for," she said.

"But you came anyway," I said, and she laughed.

Ezra rolled off me and onto her back, pulling her shirt away from her chest. "I'm sweating so bad right now."

I realized I was too. The room was way too warm, so I got to my feet and fumbled my way over to the window, opening it a little to let in the cool fall breeze.

I joined Ezra on the bed again, turning on my side so I could kiss her.

"I haven't done anything like that since I was a teenager," she said.

"I know. People skip right over dry humping and go right to sex," I said.

Ezra chuckled. "It wasn't exactly dry. I don't know why they call it that."

"You're right, but wet humping sounds…gross."

"Moist humping?" Ezra suggested and I cringed.

"That's even worse."

"Okay, I'll try and come up with something better. I'll work on it."

I was soft and dreamy from the orgasm so I decided I might as well get some of my Ezra questions answered.

"Speaking of work, what do you do?" I asked as I walked my fingers along her stomach over her shirt. "I've been dying to know."

"I'm a freelance sex columnist and sex toy blogger," she said, and I looked up in surprise.

"Oh," I said.

She tilted her head. "Was that what you were expecting?"

"I mean, I came up with all kinds of theories, but yeah, some kind of sex work was one. How the hell did you get into that?" I asked.

"I have a degree in psychology, and I want to get my master's and then become a sex therapist, specifically working with queer clients," she said. "But I needed a break from school, so I started doing this for fun and I guess people liked my writing, so I've been doing that for about a year. It's why my schedule is flexible."

This information had unlocked a whole other list of questions and wow, did I have some questions.

"Can I read your stuff?" I asked.

She shrugged one shoulder as she played with my hair. "Sure, I'm not embarrassed about it. I got the vibe you wouldn't judge me for it, but my natural instincts tell me that people are going to judge me and fuck me over, so that's why I was weird about it for a while."

"Yeah, no, that makes sense. I bet it's really interesting," I said. "You've got to be pretty unshockable to do that kind of work."

"I am," she said with a grin. "There's not much in the way of human sexuality that shocks me. Everything else about people is a puzzle."

"Well, now I'm completely intimidated. Not only are you sexy as hell, you're really smart and you know a lot about sex."

"Hey," Ezra said, taking the hand that had been making patterns on her stomach. "I'm not that smart. I've made some really dumbass decisions in my life. Trust me."

"Like agreeing to be some stranger's wedding date for a thousand bucks? Like that?" I asked.

Ezra kissed the back of my hand and smiled. "That wasn't a dumbass decision. That was one of the good decisions. Getting a matching tattoo with your ex, now that was a bad decision."

I sat up. "Where? What? Show me."

Ezra lifted up her shirt and pulled down her jeans a little bit. I looked down at what looked like half of a heart and then a circle that was sort of open.

"I get the half heart thing, but what's with the circle?"

Ezra rolled her eyes. "It's half of an infinity symbol."

"Oh," I said, trying not to laugh.

"I told you it was bad. I'm going to get a cover-up eventually, but I kind of just forget that it's there until I'm in the shower."

"I'm really trying not to judge here, Ezra," I said, looking at her.

"Go ahead, judge away."

"It's just so cliché, I'm sorry."

Ezra pulled her jeans back up and put her shirt down, hiding her skin again. I'd seen hints of other tattoos that I definitely was going to explore at some point.

"Believe me, I know. She was a cliché person."

"When did you date?" I asked. I mean, I didn't particularly want to know tons of details about her exes, but the dating history conversation was kind of standard.

"That was in college. Everything feels so intense when you're in college and you do shit you wouldn't normally do, like get a shitty couples tattoo because you think you'll be together forever. And then she moves away for grad school and you decide to do long-distance and show up for a surprise visit to find her fucking her neighbor."

I recoiled in sympathy. "Yikes, I'm so sorry."

"It was years ago. I'm good now. I told you, I don't trust people."

She had a lot of good reasons I was finding out. Why had there been so many assholes in Ezra's life? She needed to be surrounded by good people who valued her and saw how incredible she was.

"Any terrible exes in your past?" she asked.

"Not that bad. Just people who I started dating that changed their minds, or the spark fizzled out. Nothing very traumatic, actually. I mean, I cried and tried to figure out what I did wrong, but in the end, we just weren't right for each other, or we didn't have the same priorities," I said.

People just never seemed to feel as intensely about me as I did about them, and my past experiences had confirmed that many times.

"What a bunch of assholes," Ezra said, brushing her thumb across my cheek.

"Yeah, fuck them. I'd rather not talk about assholes right now."

There were still dozens of questions about Ezra's work rattling around in my brain, but she was so pretty and sexy and hot right now that they were lower priority than kissing her again. And again.

And again.

Ezra and I made out on my bed like horny teenagers and it was awesome. People really did underestimate the hotness of a make-out session and some dry humping. Or whatever we were going to call it that was better than "dry humping."

As much as I wanted to spend all night making out with her, it got late, and I had to work in the morning.

"I'm sorry," I said as I turned away to yawn for the third time.

"Hey, not a big deal. I wasn't planning on staying this long. I wasn't really planning on anything. I thought you were going to tell me to go fuck myself," she said.

"Oh, I thought about it. I practiced telling you off. And then you completely changed everything. Thanks for that," I said, but she laughed.

"If you still want to tell me off, you can," she said. I yawned again and shook my head.

"No, I'm good. I'm sure I'll have reason to yell at you at some point for some reason," I said.

Ezra got up and I followed her.

"Oh, I'm sure you will. I'm going to fuck up a lot," she said. "I might be an advice columnist, but that doesn't mean I know what the fuck I'm doing."

"At least you admit that instead of pretending like you have all the answers like some people," I said, walking her toward the door. She put her boots back on and kissed me softly before saying "bye, babe" and heading down the stairs.

Babe. I hadn't expected that either.

I couldn't help but smile as I shut the door and then turned around to find Sydney smirking in her open door.

"Looks like everything worked out."

I sighed happily. "Yeah, you could say that."

"I heard things working out too," she said, coming into the kitchen and pulling down two wine glasses. Emotional conversations and venting sessions called for tea. Gossip and sharing relationship news required wine.

"Yeah, sorry about that. I didn't know she'd be loud," I said, feeling my face going a deep red.

Sydney waved her hand and grabbed a bottle of sweet red from the fridge.

"No worries. I just put in my earbuds."

With practiced efficiency, she popped the cork and poured us each a glass, sliding one over to me.

I took a sip and looked at Sydney, who was gazing at me intently.

"Tell me everything."

Chapter Twelve

I DIDN'T TELL her everything, but I gave her enough details to satisfy her for the most part. Sydney always wanted to know the gory details, but I kept it pretty PG. Just because Sydney liked to share her sex life details with everyone, didn't mean I had to.

It was even later by the time I headed to bed, but it didn't matter if I was tired for work.

Everything was wonderful.

I floated around the kitchen the next morning and Sydney wouldn't stop shaking her head at me.

"Whipped. I've never seen someone so whipped before. Overnight."

I rolled my eyes. "I'm not whipped, and isn't that term outdated anyway?"

Sydney pointed at me with her fork. "Just be careful. If she fucks this up, I still know where to hide a body."

"You're not hiding a body," I said, shoving my plate into the dishwasher and then grabbing my lunch from the fridge.

"You say that now, but I'm here if you need it. I've got your back."

"Thanks, I think," I said, kissing her cheek before heading downstairs to work.

~

I WASN'T sure what kind of texting frequency we're on now, but I figured it couldn't hurt to say good morning Ezra sent around nine-thirty.

Good morning. Text whenever you want. I check my phone a lot during the day and my boss doesn't mind. How's your work? I responded.

I was dying to know what she did all day. I'd searched her name online to try and find her column this morning, but hadn't gotten any hits, which made sense if she wrote under a pseudonym.

She sent me a picture of her laptop screen with her hand covering most of it.

Most of my work is writing about sex, but sometimes I pick up other jobs to pay the bills. Right now I'm writing copy for a new website. Not glamorous, but it's steady.

That sounded like what Paige did. I wondered if she might have some leads on jobs that Ezra could pick up if Paige's schedule was too full.

I sent her a picture of the new stock I was organizing.

Exciting, I know.

Books are exciting, in my opinion she responded and that made me smile.

"How's it going back here?" Erin said, taking a minute to check in with me.

"Good. The books on the shipping list actually match the books we've gotten, so we're ahead of the game already."

She laughed at that. We'd had a shipment recently that was supposed to be several new cookbooks, but we'd ended up with a bunch of manuals on how to perform an exorcism and the company still didn't know how the mix-up happened and told us we could keep the exorcism books, but Kendra had ended up donating them. I was fairly sure they were going to end up at the recycling center eventually.

"Good. Just let me know if you need anything," she said.

"Will do," I said, but she paused in the doorway.

"Did you cut your hair or something?" she asked. My hair was loosely tied back from my face. I hadn't had time to do anything elaborate with it this morning.

"No," I said, touching my hair.

"Oh, well, you look like you got a facial or a massage or something. You look glowy."

My hand moved to my cheek and I felt myself blush. "Thanks. Must be my new skincare regimen."

"Well, whatever it is, keep doing it."

She went back out to the front and I couldn't stop grinning.

~

EZRA SHOWED up for lunch and I'd had a suspicion she would, so I'd packed extra just in case.

"Jumbo meatballs and veggie curry rice?" I asked her when we went back to the office.

"Sure," she said. "That sounds great."

I put both containers in the microwave to heat up as she sat in one of the other chairs.

"Sorry, this isn't that romantic, we can go upstairs if you want."

Ezra shook her head and leaned back in her chair.

"This is fine. It's like being behind the curtain."

I laughed and the microwave dinged. I passed the container to Ezra and handed her a fork and a napkin.

"I feel like I haven't seen you in forever, but it was literally last night," I said as we ate.

"Work has really been a challenge today because I can't focus. I'm sure you can guess why," she said, cutting one of the meatballs in half with her fork.

"Yeah, I haven't been firing on all cylinders either."

We both smiled at each other and I really wanted to dive across the desk between us and kiss her and push her up against the door and maybe sneak in a little fingering. Who cared about food?

"I think I'm going to come to book club," she said. "Inspired by you telling me to be brave, I've decided that I should put myself out there more."

"That's awesome. I promise you're going to have a good time," I said.

"I'll hold you to that," she said.

"If you absolutely hate it and need to bail, just tell me 'candy nipples' and then sneak out the back."

Ezra threw back her head and laughed. "Okay, I will."

My lunch break passed all to quickly and soon I was shoving the empty containers back into my bag and Ezra was giving me a soft kiss.

"If I finish my work tonight, do you want to have dinner or something?" she asked.

"Yeah, definitely. I'm supposed to cook tonight for Syd, but I'm sure she wouldn't mind if you joined us."

Ezra nodded. "Yeah, sure, I'll let you know."

She gave me another kiss before heading out the back door and I went back to work.

~

"IS it okay if Ezra joins us?" I asked Syd as I pulled out everything I needed to make dinner. Before I'd talked to Ezra, I'd planned on just making something easy, like carbonara, but now I wanted to impress Ezra, so I was going to bake some chicken and make my spinach and butternut squash tart for a side dish.

"Yeah, no problem," she said, grabbing a seltzer from the fridge and popping it open. "Just as long as you don't abandon me for her, we'll be good."

That was something I'd thought about, even before Ezra. How to balance spending time with Sydney and my other friends, and how to balance a romantic relationship. Plus, there was my job and my reading were also a priority. And then the random demands my family placed on me and there weren't enough hours in the day to breathe.

"You know I wouldn't do that," I said, hugging her from behind.

"I know. You're good. And I am happy for you, Joy. Ezra seems great, and she's really into you, which shows good judgment. As long as she doesn't hurt you, I'm cool with her."

I waved her off and went back to cooking. "Yeah, yeah, I know."

～

EVERYTHING WAS in the oven and still cooking when Ezra showed up.

"Hey," she said, holding something behind her back.

"What do you have?" I asked immediately.

"I wanted to bring you something like flowers, but then I saw this at the store when I was getting groceries and I had to get it."

She revealed a flowerpot that was filled with something bright red and wrapped in cellophane.

"Candy apples?" I asked when I looked closer.

"It's a bouquet of candy apples. There are three of them, so one for each of us," she said, handing it to me.

"This is so nice, thank you," I said.

Sydney sidled over.

"Bringing treats and including the roommate. Well played," she said.

"Sydney, don't be weird," I said, admiring the gift and then setting it on the counter. They were almost too pretty to eat.

"So, uh, dinner will be ready in fifteen minutes. Did you want a drink?" I asked, opening the fridge to show her what we had.

"Seltzer is fine," she said, and I grabbed her a can and one for myself.

"I'm going to go back to the living room, but don't forget I'm here," Sydney said.

"We couldn't possibly forget. You wouldn't let us," I said.

Sydney just flipped her middle finger up and flopped on the couch.

Ezra sat on one of the stools and watched me as I got out the plates.

"Can I do anything to help?" she asked.

"Nope, I've got this. How was writing today?"

"I finished the writing for the website, which is good. It was all very dry and boring, so I just had to put my head down and get through it," she said.

"You remember Esme, that we met at the bar?" I asked.

"Of course."

"Her wife, Paige, is a content creator and she does that kind of stuff too. If you ever need more jobs, I'm sure she'd be happy to maybe share some leads with you," I said.

"Oh, I don't want to take her jobs," Ezra said.

"No, it's fine. She's always saying that she doesn't have enough time to do all the jobs she gets contacted for. She's also gotten pickier now that she's established herself, so there are smaller jobs that she passes on all the time."

Ezra sipped her seltzer and told me more about her writing, but it wasn't as interesting as her other work.

"When did you figure out what you wanted to do?" I asked. I was being purposefully vague in front of Sydney. I hadn't told her about Ezra's job since I wasn't sure if she wanted me to share it with anyone else.

"I really had no idea. I'd just gone into psychology because it seemed interesting, and then I had a professor that really impacted my life. She sat down with me and talked about her work and I ended up working as a TA for her my last two years and she's really the reason I chose the path I did," she said.

The timer went off and I pulled everything out of the oven.

"That smells incredible," Ezra said, closing her eyes and inhaling.

"Thanks. It's a baked chicken and then a fall spinach and squash tart."

"I'm sure it's going to be delicious," Ezra said. Sydney finally wandered into the kitchen for food and we decided to eat in the living room for comfort.

"I guess that means I get the chair," Sydney grumbled. Our couch was tiny and could really only fit two and a half people comfortably, which was usually me, Syd, and Clementine.

Tonight it was me, Ezra, Syd, and a clingy Clementine.

"This is really good," Ezra said after she'd had a bite each of the chicken and the tart.

"Seriously good. I know you're showing off for Ezra, but since I also benefit, I approve," Syd said.

"Thanks," I said to Ezra. I didn't bother responding to Syd.

Ezra asked for seconds, and I was happy to get them for her.

Syd took her plate over to the sink and then came back to the living room.

"I'm going to read in my room. Please don't fuck on the couch," she said. Ezra choked on a piece of chicken and I handed her the can of seltzer so she could clear her throat.

"Very nice, Sydney," I called as Syd shut her door. Clementine immediately went to investigate and meowed at the door until Syd opened it up and let him in. He was going to want to come out in about five minutes.

Ezra finished her second portion and took her dishes to the kitchen.

"Did you want tea or coffee or something?" I asked.

"No, I'm fine with seltzer," she said. "Do you mind if I have another one?"

"No, go for it. Take whatever you want," I said.

Ezra got another can and brought me one.

"When do I get to see your house?" I asked as she popped the top. "Is it secret?"

"No, it's not secret. It's just not that nice," she said. I remembered when Layne had started getting interested in Honor and Honor had been secretive about where she lived because she was ashamed.

"Listen, this is no penthouse. The hot water goes out all the time, the sink leaks randomly, the windows don't shut when it's hot, and we get ants every summer," I said. It was still a pretty decent apartment for Arrowbridge, which was mostly homes for sale and neither I or Syd could afford that.

"You probably know where it is. I'm living in this little garage apartment over on Wilson Street," she said.

"Oh, yeah, I know where that is," I said. "I'd love to see it, if you want to show me."

"Sure, we'll do that sometime," she said, getting cagey. I let the subject drop.

"Do you want your candy apple now?" Ezra asked.

"Yes, please." She went and brought it back over and pulled the third apple out of the pot, heading to Sydney's door and knocking.

"Yes?" Syd said, opening the door a crack.

"I thought you might want this," Ezra said, holding up the candy apple.

"You thought right," Syd said, snatching it out of her hand and closing the door again.

"Just ignore her," I said, unwrapping my apple. The candy coating was shiny and thick.

"Let's face it, the reason you eat a candy apple is so you can munch on the coating and feel less guilt because there's fruit underneath," I said.

"I don't think you should feel any guilt about candy apples," Ezra said, unwrapping hers.

"Cheers to that," I said, and we gently tapped our apples together. It seemed like we were toasting all kinds of things, but it felt right to celebrate little things like candy apples.

The coating cracked as I tried to bite into it, and I realized we both needed paper towels so we didn't get candy shards all over the floor for Clementine to find or get stuck on his fur.

I ripped off a few and handed them to Ezra.

"Thanks," she said, her lips already red from the candy coating. Her mouth looked more delicious than my apple at the moment.

I held my apple out of the way and made sure I wasn't going to crash into hers as I leaned forward and captured her lips, licking the sweetness from them.

"Sorry," I said. "Couldn't help myself."

"Don't apologize," Ezra said, and then she kissed me.

"Shit," she said, and I realized that her apple was stuck in my hair.

"It's okay," I said, laughing as she tried to pull it out without ripping out my hair. "Come on."

We both walked in tandem to the bathroom and I stuck my head near the sink as Ezra ruined her candy apple to get my hair free.

"You should probably wash it," she said.

"Okay. Want to help me?" I asked, feeling brazen.

"Are you sure you're ready for that?"

"We can wear our underwear," I said. Maybe the sugar was making me bold.

"If you're sure," she said, dumping the now-ruined apple in the sink, red coloring dripping from it like blood.

I pulled my shirt over my head and thanked my presence of mind I'd had this morning to put on a matching bra and underwear set that wasn't old or stained or shabby.

This set wasn't fancy, but it was new and pretty, white with little pink flowers.

Ezra pulled her shirt over her head and I wasn't shocked to find a simple black bra, and matching boyshorts when she pulled off her jeans.

"Finally, I get to see more of your tattoos," I said, circling around her. She had the sleeve on her arm, and then the one on her hip that I could just barely see, but she also had her back done, and a huge thigh piece.

"Will you tell me what they all mean? If they mean something. Tattoos don't have to be significant."

I didn't have any of my own, but I'd always thought they were really beautiful.

"Sure," Ezra said as I turned on the water and stepped into the shower. She followed me, letting me get under the spray first so I could deal with my sticky hair.

She handed the bottle of shampoo to me.

"Thanks," I said, squeezing some into my hand and then working it through my hair, paying attention to where the candy apple had been.

Ezra watched me, as if she wasn't really sure what she was

doing in the shower with me. So I turned around and looked at her over my shoulder.

"Can you help me?" I asked. It wasn't like I needed help washing my hair, but having Ezra massage my scalp sounded great right now.

She pressed her fingers into my hair and circled them.

"Mmm, that feels really good," I said. She did the top of my head and moved back, making sure that none of the soap got into my eyes before moving down and massaging my neck.

"You've got great fingers," I said. I'd noticed those fingers right away, and not just because of the tattoos.

I wanted those fingers all over me, inside me. That wasn't the point of this shower, so I kept my fantasies to myself as Ezra helped me rinse my hair.

"Conditioner?" she asked.

"Yes, please," I said, and she worked that through my hair as well.

"Your hair is so shiny, I thought you would have some really expensive treatments that have been blessed by monks or something," she said.

It was true, my hair was one of my best physical attributes. I didn't do much to keep it nice. I just got trims regularly and made sure I detangled it with a wide-toothed comb and didn't put too much product in it.

"No," I said. "Just good genes."

My mom and sisters also had great hair. My dad was bald, so I guess those genes didn't come from his side.

"How often do you cut your undercut?" I asked.

"About every few weeks. My hair grows fast, so I had to learn how to do it myself or else I'd be stuck going and getting it done constantly. A lot of hair places don't like doing undercuts," she said, and I switched positions with her so she could get under the hot water and I could let the conditioner work.

Ezra finally took her hair down and tipped her head back under the spray.

"Sometimes I think about cutting it all off, but I like having some to put up. I don't know why," she said.

"It's a good look for you," I said. "I mean, you pull it off."

"Thanks," she said, her cheeks going pink from the compliment.

I grabbed the shampoo bottle and held it up.

"Your turn. But you might have to duck down a little bit." With her being taller, she would either have to crouch, or I'd need a stool.

Ezra turned around and then bent her knees until I could reach the top of her head. I washed her hair and couldn't help but run my hands over her undercut.

"You do a really good job of making the back even, I'm impressed," I said. I know if I had clippers, I would not be able to get the same perfect line.

"Lots of practice," she said, standing up to rinse.

We swapped back again so I could wash out the conditioner and then added it to Ezra's hair.

Once our hair was clean, I didn't want to get out of the shower, even though we were using up the hot water.

"Come here," she said, using my hips to pull me closer before she kissed me under the water.

I couldn't breathe, but it didn't really matter.

Ezra backed me up until my back hit the shower wall. I let out a little gasp that made her smile.

Her clever fingers wound into my hair and used it to expose my neck that she licked and kissed and sucked. I knew she was leaving marks, but did I care? No. Let her mark me. I'd wear them proudly.

Ezra pulled back with a groan and my eyes flew open. What happened?"

"We should stop," she said, her voice breathless.

"Why?" I asked. We were just getting started.

"Because if I don't stop now, I don't know if I can," she said, closing her eyes.

I didn't want her to stop, but there was a teeny tiny voice of reason that said that stopping might be a good idea. We had literally just agreed to start seeing each other and hopping straight into sex could be a bad idea.

"You're right," I said, my voice husky. I turned off the shower and reached for my towel.

"Give me just a second." I pulled an extra towel out of the little linen cabinet for Ezra.

We dried off and then I wasn't sure what to do.

"I can throw your stuff in the dryer and give you a robe," I said.

"That works," Ezra said, using the towel to blot her hair.

One of the huge selling points of this apartment, along with the location, was the fact that it had a washer and dryer in the closet next to the bathroom.

Still wrapped in my towel, I got Ezra a robe and she put it on before stripping out of her underwear and handing it to me.

"Be right back," I said.

"I'll meet you in your room," she said.

I put her stuff in the dryer and dashed to my room, still dripping.

Ezra was perched on my bed in her robe, flushed and damp and lovely.

"Um, just give me a second to change," I said, pulling a new outfit out of my drawers.

"I'll just turn around," Ezra said.

"Thanks," I said, waiting for her before I dropped the towel and got dressed as fast as I could, not forgetting that she was completely naked under her robe. My robe, actually.

"I'm decent," I said, and she turned around.

"You're gorgeous," she said as I tried to get as much water

out of my hair as I could before putting just a little bit of styling cream and grabbing my comb to go through the tangles.

"Thanks," I said.

"Want me to help you?" she asked, holding her hand out for the comb.

"Sure. Just be careful."

"I will be," she said.

I sat down on the edge of the bed and Ezra sat behind me, starting at the ends and working her way up. If she hit a snag, she teased it out gently before moving on.

"I like this," she said, her voice soft. "Just being with you."

"I like being with you, too." This comfort was so new, but it was so right.

"I like kissing you, obviously, but this is great too. I'd forgotten how nice it can be to just be with another person," she said.

I closed my eyes and reveled in her touch.

The apartment was quiet until I heard a voice.

"Why is there a candy apple in the bathroom sink?"

Ezra snorted. "I guess we forgot to clean that up."

"Oops," I said. "Just throw it away!" I yelled through the door at Sydney.

"I'm not touching your sex apple!"

I got up from the bed and cracked my bedroom door. "I don't know what the hell you think we were doing with that apple, but we were not having sex with it. If you don't want to trash it, I'll go out and grab it later."

Sydney smirked at me. "I wouldn't care even if you were using it for sex. Go get some, my love," she said.

I made a disgusted sound and closed the door.

"I support your sex life!" Syd yelled. I turned around to find Ezra fighting a smile.

"Having a sex-positive friend is a good thing to have," she said.

"Yes, but there is such a thing as being a little too positive. I think she's in a slump so she's meddling in my life because it's more fun than dealing with her own stuff," I said, flopping down on the bed again. "Anyway, I don't want to talk about my roommate's sex life. I'd rather talk to you."

Ezra chuckled and adjusted the robe.

"I like talking with you. It's easier than I thought it would be. I'm really out of practice, though. I'm so good at listening to other people and making it all about them, but when it comes to sharing some of myself, I'm rusty."

"I think you're doing great so far," I said, leaning over to kiss her. Her underwear was probably dry, but I really liked seeing her in my robe. It was doing all kinds of things for me.

"It's getting late, and I know you have to be up for work tomorrow," she said.

"It's not that late," I said. "Unless you were sick of being with me." It was still hard to read Ezra that way.

"Hey," she said, grabbing the front of my shirt. "I'm not sick of hanging out with you. Not even a little bit."

She kissed me and I forgot everything we'd been talking about.

～

EVENTUALLY EZRA'S CLOTHES DRIED, and she got dressed. I tried not to pout too much.

"I have a bunch of deadlines tomorrow, so I might not see you," she said. "But I'll be at book club on Thursday night. I think I'm going to be finished by then."

"Really?" I asked.

"Yeah, it's a good book. You have excellent taste, Joy."

I beamed. That was one of the highest compliments.

"Thanks," I said, giving her another kiss before following her out of the bedroom. Sydney was in the living room on the couch with her candy apple, watching a reunion episode of a reality show. Everyone on the stage was screaming at each other as the host looked on with glee.

"This is a good one, you're going to want to see it," Syd said. "Thanks for the apple, Ezra."

"You're welcome," she said as we paused at the door.

"Text me when you take a break if you want," I said.

"I will," she said, touching my chin and tilting my face up to place a soft kiss to my mouth.

"Bye, Joy," she said.

"Bye, Ezra," I said, missing her already. She walked down the stairs and then waved before heading out the door to the parking lot.

I closed the door and leaned against it.

"Look at you, all dreamy eyed," Sydney teased.

"Shut up and start that episode over. You said you weren't going to watch it without me," I said, pointing an accusatory finger at her.

"It's not my fault you were too busy banging your hot girlfriend," she said as I sat down on the couch and grabbed the remote from her.

"For the last time, Ezra and I were not banging," I said, starting the episode over.

"You will be soon," Sydney said. "I swear the air around you two is combustible."

"Shut up," I said, shoving her shoulder. "We're still figuring shit out."

Sydney looked at me, tilting her head to the side. "Combustible looks good on you."

Chapter Thirteen

I DIDN'T SEE Ezra the next day, as she'd said, but she did send me a few pictures of her working, wearing black-framed glasses that made her five thousand percent hotter, if that was even possible. I wanted to ask her why she didn't wear them all the time, but figured they were blue-light glasses to protect her eyes from the computer glare.

"Hi Joy," a friendly voice said, and I looked up to find McKenna, a Castleton resident that taught yoga.

"Hey, how's it going? What brings you to Arrowbridge?" I asked.

"I was just wondering if you could put up my flyer for private yoga classes in the window," she said, holding up a sheet of paper she'd pulled from a folder.

"Absolutely," I said, taking it from her.

"Thanks, I really appreciate it. I love teaching classes online, but private clients really help keep a steady income."

I nodded and found some tape in one of the drawers behind the counter and she helped me find a good spot where people would see it.

"I support all freelancers," I said. "You've gotta do what you need to in this economy."

"We appreciate that," McKenna said, and pulled her phone out of the pocket of her yoga pants. She always looked like she'd come right from the yoga mat.

She smiled as she read the message and then put her phone away.

"Hey, do you have anything new for a little boy who loves superheroes while I'm here?" she asked.

McKenna's girlfriend, Piper, had a young son from her marriage that McKenna was going through the process to officially adopt. His dad was out of the picture, so McKenna had stepped right into her role as second mom.

"I've got you, come with me," I said, taking her back to a particular shelf of books.

"I can't wait until he's older and can read the comics. I've been searching and buying vintage ones for him online," she said.

"These will hopefully keep him going for a little while," I said, handing her a stack.

"You're the best," she said, following me to the counter so I could check her out.

"Thanks for the books and the help with the poster," she said.

"Anytime. I'll see you for Non Book Club, right?"

"See you then," she said, waving and then heading out the door.

The Castleton Crew had started their own book club, and Kendra let them have our space to meet once a month. Every now and then Kendra wasn't available to help with those nights, so I'd stepped in and had made sure they had chairs, and everything was set up and supervised. They weren't a rowdy bunch, so it wasn't hard.

Ezra sent me a quick video of her making coffee. I watched

the thing multiple times, trying to get a good view of her apartment. I was dying to know how it was decorated. Sydney and I had sort of smashed our styles together. I was a fan of soft colors and pillows and Sydney was more industrial and rustic and somehow it sort of worked. Our style was often limited by our budget, so we settled for items from discount stores or what people were giving away online. My mom had tried to offload a bunch of things when she and Dad had downsized, but I'd managed to get away with just taking a table and a few lamps. The couch had been a suede monstrosity that was better suited to the dump than a living room, but Mom was convinced it had held its value and was still worth money. She'd been a little salty when she hadn't had any offers at her asking price at the moving sale. She still ranted about it if she had a second glass of wine.

I sent her back a quick video of the shop during the lull. Kendra was working on bookkeeping in the back, and social media management.

If you've got time, pick out a book for me she sent.

What kind of book? I asked, knowing she probably wasn't going to give me much of an idea. I had to admit, it was kind of fun to let someone curate their book collection.

You pick. Find me something with lots of adventure she responded.

That was something, so I got up and headed right for the fantasy section. While this wasn't a queer-only bookstore, we did stock a large selection of queer books, and since Ezra hadn't told me she didn't want non-queer material, I plucked a really gorgeous and intense historical fantasy set in China. Hopefully that would satisfy her need for adventure.

I set a copy behind the counter for later. I also grabbed a soft and sweet romance with a green cover and a punny title about knitting and added that. She'd need it after the other book.

Kendra poked her head out of the office. "Hey, I completely forgot we need to do a new set of Blind Date books, can you grab some for me?" she asked.

"Yeah, no problem."

One of the most fun things we did at the store was Blind Date with a Book. One of us would pick a book off the shelves, wrap it up, and write a quick description on the front that didn't give away what the book was. Readers would choose a book without knowing what it would be. We had quite a few loyal customers that absolutely loved to come in whenever we added more, so I even made some picks with them in mind.

After a little bit of thinking, I picked five books and gave them to Kendra for approval.

"Nice," she said, looking through. "Good selection. If you want to wrap them up and then do the blurbs, go for it," she said. "I'm in the weeds with this social media stuff."

"We really should hire someone who knows what they're doing with that," I said. It was something I had said before.

Kendra sighed and rubbed her eyes. She looked tired.

"I know. I keep hoping that some college student in graphic design is going to wander in and ask for an internship or something," she said.

"Yeah, I don't think that's going to happen. Why don't you ask Hollis or Sasha? I'm sure they'd know someone. Or even Piper. She does brand consulting, or something like that, right?" Hollis worked as a graphic designer making book covers and promo for authors, and Sasha worked as an author assistant and sometimes did graphic design herself. Piper worked with huge brands on their marketing campaigns, but maybe she'd give Kendra a little consult or know where to start looking for someone to hire.

"I know, I've thought about it. I guess I just thought I could handle it and life is teaching me that no, I can't."

"I can help more," I said. I'd done a few things for the

social account, like taking pictures of displays and doing some tours and day in the life of a bookseller videos, but I could definitely do more.

"No, it's fine. You do enough already. I'm going to ask around and see if we can at least get someone part time to give us a boost," she said.

"Let me know if you want me to ask too," I said, feeling guilty that I'd been slacking.

"Thanks, you're the best," she said. "And now I need coffee." She pushed to her feet and went to the stock room slash break room to refuel on caffeine.

I immediately started walking around the shop, taking pictures and wondering what I could post on social media. In between customers, I worked on the social media conundrum for the rest of the day, and by the time I headed back upstairs, I was exhausted.

"Will Ezra be joining us for dinner?" Syd asked as I set my bag down and yawned.

"No, she has to work. She's going to be at book club tomorrow night, though."

"Joining book club? This is serious," she said, flipping a potsticker.

"Shut up, it's not that big of a deal." I slid onto one of the stools and watched her cook.

"How was work?" I asked as she flipped another potsticker and then checked on the pot of soup she had going on another burner. Potsticker soup was one of the best comfort meals, so Syd must have had a not so good day.

Figuring she might need a hand, I got up to fetch the spinach and green onions for finishing the soup.

"Work was work," she said. "I think I need a vacation."

"Then you should take one. Go rent a cabin somewhere. Read lots of books and sit in the bathtub and order delivery."

Syd closed her eyes and sighed in pleasure.

"Or I could bring a fleet of vibrators and lube and masturbate for hours," she said, and I thought I was going to choke on my own air.

"Syd! I don't need to hear about your masturbation habits," I said.

Syd faced me and rolled her eyes. "Like I don't hear you in your room."

It was true. The apartment didn't have much in the way of soundproofing and there had been many times when I'd heard more of Syd and she'd heard more of me than we wanted.

"So you're back on your sex hiatus? At least your sex hiatus of being with other people?"

Syd shrugged. "I don't know. That last attempt has left me scared to try again for some reason."

She seemed down and I gave her a hug. "You'll be back to your old sexy self soon, I'm sure," I said.

She let out a grunt and turned off the potstickers before tossing them in the soup with the spinach and green onions before handing me a bowl.

"How was work today for you?" she asked.

"Kendra's stressed out about the social media accounts for the bookstore. I told her she needs to hire someone, and I know she doesn't exactly have the budget for it, but none of us really know what the hell we're doing in that department. I mean, I can take pictures and post them and come up with some captions, but I don't have the skills to make clever videos and so forth."

Doing a quick trendy dance with your friends was one thing, but trying to keep up and make it professional and relevant to the store was something for an actual expert. My degree was in English, not marketing or graphic design.

"I'm sure there's some extremely online teenager around here who would want to pick up some extra cash that would want to get some job experience," Syd said.

"I think so."

She did seem better after her first bowl of soup, and even better after we discovered a new show on streaming that sounded just trashy enough for both of us.

Ezra texted me later that night. It was a picture of our book club book.

Finished just in time. It was so cute. I couldn't stop smiling she sent.

I'm excited for you to come and meet everyone. Don't be too intimidated, we're a very chill group I responded.

I'm trying to be chill about it myself she sent.

You'll be fine. And if you need to, you can always yell 'candy nipples!' and I'll hurry you out the back door I responded.

Perfect plan she sent.

I can't tell if you're kidding or not. I think it's an excellent plan I replied.

Joy. I think yelling 'candy nipples' in front of a bunch of strangers is more embarrassing than having to make small talk with them she sent.

I mean, she had a point.

Okay well maybe just whisper it in my ear if you need to tap out I responded.

That sounds a little more reasonable she sent.

We messaged back and forth like that until it was really time for me to get to bed. Ezra said her day had been productive, but that she still had a bunch of work to get done tomorrow, so she wouldn't be able to take lunch with me but would show up a little early for book club. I'd forgotten that I needed to run to Castleton to get the cake during my lunch, so that was fine with me. Still, it might have been fun to bring Ezra on the cake excursion. I was petrified of dropping it. I'd seen too many videos of people dropping cakes online.

I'll see you tomorrow Joy she sent as my eyes started to close. The light of my phone was bright in my dark room.

See you tomorrow Ezra

~

"I'M sorry I can't help you unload," Martha, the owner of Sweet's Sweets said. Normally I would have gotten the cake from her daughter, Linley, but she was still on maternity leave with her daughter, Georgia.

"Kendra is going to help me," I said. "I'm not taking any chances."

I gently shut the door of the car.

"Thanks so much, you're the best. Say hi to Linley and Georgia for me," I said.

"Of course," Martha said, tapping the roof of the car. "Let me know if it's a crowd pleaser."

"I know it will be," I said, and got in the driver's seat.

~

"I DON'T KNOW how people drive around with children in the car," I said as I opened the back passenger door and prayed that the cake had made it in one piece.

Kendra laughed. "It's not that bad, and that's what car seats are for. They don't make cake seats."

"They should. You should suggest that to Linley. Could be a whole new market for them. Cake protectors."

Kendra snorted and carefully drew the box out as I reached for the other end. We'd already propped the back door open.

"Slowly," I said as we creeped along the sidewalk and then into the bookstore.

I didn't fully exhale until the cake was in the fridge in the break room. Kendra shut the door and pretended to wipe sweat from her brow.

"Now we just have to get it in the table in one piece," I said.

"That's a problem for us in a few hours," she said, patting my shoulder. "Go finish your break."

I ran upstairs and had some leftover soup before going back to work. The rest of the day was spent handling customers and prepping for book club. I'd probably gone overboard this month, but that had been due to the wedding stress that Ezra had miraculously alleviated.

I owed her the next third of the payment on Saturday and every time I thought about it, I felt gross, so I was trying not to think about it. She hadn't mentioned it, but I wasn't going to go back on what we'd agreed to now that we were kind of dating. Were we dating? I didn't actually know for sure.

Kendra and I finally got the cake onto the table in its place of honor and I couldn't help but clap from excitement.

"You've gone above and beyond, Joy, really," Kendra said, looking around. I'd gotten balloons that looked like rings and a JUST MARRIED banner and rainbow plates to go with the inside of the cake. I also had champagne and sparkling apple juice and plastic flutes for drinking instead of the regular plastic cups.

"Thanks," I said.

"I'm going to head out, thanks for staying, but I promised Theo I'd help watch Mia and Oliver with her tonight. Their parents are going on a very quick, but much-deserved getaway for a few days. You'll probably see them all in here tomorrow. I know Mia is dying to come and 'help' me in the stock room for some reason. She really thinks it's going to be like Santa's workshop and she's going to be so disappointed when she sees what it's really like."

I laughed and waved goodbye to her as she headed out the

door just as Ezra walked in. She said hello to Kendra and then came right over to me.

"Ta-da," I said, striking a little pose. "What do you think?" I didn't know why I cared so much. I just didn't want her to think it was too much or too tacky or too something.

"Wow, it looks great. Very festive," she said, leaning down to give me a kiss. It felt like forever since she'd kissed me, but it hadn't even been two days.

"Thanks," I said. "Would you like a glass of sparkling cider?"

"Yes, please," she said, and I opened the bottle, pouring a glass for her and one for myself.

"You did a lot of work," Ezra said, looking at the chairs and the decor. The only food so far was the cake, since some of the members like to contribute by bringing something. Layne was bringing a charcuterie board with cheese cut into diamond shapes, she'd said, sending me pictures of the cutter she'd gotten. She'd also made rainbow chocolate-dipped pretzels, so I wasn't the only one who had gone overboard with the theme.

"How was work today?" I asked Ezra as we waited for more people to arrive.

"Busy," she said. "I had three deadlines to meet and I thought I was going to lose my mind, but everything is done so I can take a breather for a few days. It kind of comes all at once like that."

I asked more about her work, but she started getting monosyllabic, so I figured she wasn't comfortable talking about it where someone might overhear, so I started messing with the chairs. Layne and Honor arrived, followed quickly by a few other members, and then Sydney.

The volume in the bookshop increased and I had to help people with setting up the food and making sure we had enough chairs and catching up with everyone that I hadn't seen since last book club. I lost track of Ezra, but I saw her standing with Honor and talking while Layne passed out plates and napkins.

That was an interesting combination, but Ezra didn't seem to be screaming "candy nipples" or sending up the bat signal or anything, so I left her to her own devices until it was time to sit down and start.

"Okay, who wants to share their impressions of the book first?" I asked. We kept things pretty informal, but I did try to keep the discussion going with questions I'd written ahead of time. Sometimes we'd go off on a tangent, but that was fine. There was no set format, and if anyone didn't want to contribute, they could just sit and observe. No one was forced to talk if they didn't want to. We had at least two members that I'd never heard speak, but they'd come up to me after and say what they thought.

Honor hadn't spoken her first meeting, but my theory was she'd been too busy staring at Layne.

We had lovely discussion and I saw Ezra nodding intently, but she didn't say anything. We wound down and I cut the cake to applause.

"I feel like I need to smash it in someone's face," I said.

"Don't look at me," Ezra said, putting both hands up.

"Don't worry, I wouldn't," I said. With someone more comfortable I might, but I didn't want her to run away. That didn't stop me from imagining, just for a second, Ezra in a white suit standing next to me with our wedding cake between us.

"Who wants the first piece?" I asked, and Layne helped me distribute it as everyone stuffed their faces and exclaimed how good it was.

Finally, there were two pieces left, one for me, and one for Ezra.

"Cake?" I asked.

"Always," she said, taking the plate from me.

We stood together at the edge of the rest of the group.

"So? What do you think?" I asked.

"It is a nice group. You're not upset that I didn't talk, are you?" she asked.

"No, of course not. Just being here is enough," I said.

Ezra studied me as if she was trying to see if I was telling the truth.

"Thanks, that means a lot," she said.

"I saw you talking to Honor earlier," I said.

"She seems nice. I'd seen her once before when I was out driving around and stopped to get some coffee in Castleton. She'd been ahead of me in line at the café. She seems very... together," she said.

"She is. I've never seen her with a hair out of place, and I've seen her after she swam in the ocean. She's like, disturbingly pretty," I said.

Ezra turned her head to the side. "Is that your type, Joy?"

I shook my head. "No way. I like someone with a little more edge to them. Someone with knuckle tattoos, perhaps," I said, tapping her hand with my fork. "That kind of pretty does nothing for me."

Ezra leaned closer to me, and I could smell that spicy scent from her skin.

"That's good to know," she said.

"I'm way more into goth trombone players," I said, keeping my face serious.

"If you tell anyone else about that, I will murder you," Ezra said, but she was laughing.

Chapter Fourteen

EZRA CAME UPSTAIRS with me and Sydney and Layne and Honor to hang out after book club, and I wanted to ask her if she wanted to stay over, but she gave me a soft kiss and said she'd bring me lunch tomorrow and I should get some sleep. I was exhausted from organizing book club, so she did have a point.

Ezra showed up with my rainbow wrap, and we ate them upstairs in my apartment and made out a little.

"You're going to make me late," I said in between kisses.

"So?" she said, her finger flicking the button of my jeans.

"You are a bad influence. I'm going to tell my boss on you," I said.

"I think your boss will support me," Ezra said, licking her way down my neck.

Her hand slid into my jeans, but over the fabric of my underwear. We hadn't gotten this close since that time in the shower and that was nearly a week ago. In lieu of Ezra getting me off, I'd had to take care of things on my own and my two favorite vibrators had gotten quite a workout, as had my hand.

"Ezra," I whined, and she removed her hand, which was actually the opposite of what I really wanted.

"How about I come over tonight?" Ezra said, sighing and then zipping my jeans up again.

"Or I could go to your place. You don't have a roommate, right?" I asked.

She shook her head. "Nope. It's just me."

"Just you sounds perfect," I said, sucking on her bottom lip before forcing myself to get to my feet. "I love Sydney, but having a roommate isn't always the most convenient."

"Tonight then," Ezra said, running her fingers through my hair. "How about I pick you up after work? You can stay over and then I'll drive us to the bridal shower."

Honestly, that sounded ideal. I'd just have to remember to pack my outfit with my stuff. And go through my underwear to find the sexiest pair.

"Since you're driving and we're staying at your place, how about I grab some groceries and cook dinner for us?" I asked.

"You don't have to do that. I figured we could just get pizza from Nick's." While I loved Nick's pizza, especially because he and his husband Antonio were always flirting in the kitchen, I wanted to impress Ezra.

"No, I want to cook for you," I said, mentally going through my recipes. Something warm and cozy, definitely. Pumpkin risotto and chicken thighs with brussels sprouts and bacon. Both were crowd pleasers I'd made enough times that I could whip them up pretty easily in someone else's kitchen.

Ezra closed her eyes and smiled as she opened them. "That sounds really nice, Joy."

"You have a baking dish and a large skillet, right?" I asked.

She blinked at me once. "I have a frying pan, will that work? I definitely don't have a baking pan."

I'd had a feeling that might be the case.

"No problem, I'll just bring mine." And I'd bring my skillet as well, since I didn't know how big her pan was and I wanted to make enough so she could have leftovers.

Ezra kissed me suddenly and then pulled back, gazing into my eyes. "This might sound corny, but you're a treasure, Joy Greene."

Being with Ezra made me feel treasured. Valued. She was interested in what I had to say, and I never felt like I was boring her, or talking too much.

"So are you, Ezra Evans," I said, kissing her back.

∽

THAT NIGHT when Ezra picked me up, I had an overnight bag with pajamas, my toothbrush, my outfit for the bridal shower, and a bag with my skillet and a baking pan in it.

"Let me help you," she said, rushing over to take the bag with the pan and the dish in it.

"Thanks. I still need to go to the grocery store. I'll run in and you can just wait for me," I said as I slid into the passenger seat.

Ezra gave me a weird look. "Why would I wait for you?"

"Grocery shopping isn't that exciting," I said.

Ezra grabbed my hand and kissed it. "Going grocery shopping with you wouldn't be boring."

My body warmed in a way that had nothing to do with the temperature inside the car.

"Besides, I realized I have next to nothing to feed you with tomorrow morning, so I need to get some things too."

The bridal shower was mid-afternoon, so Anna was serving little quiches and squash and pumpkin soup and cookies shaped like leaves to go with the theme.

Ezra pulled into the lot of the Yellow Roof Grocery store and got some reusable grocery bags from her trunk.

"I came prepared," she said, holding them up.

I couldn't say why, but she looked so cute and sexy holding those grocery bags with a smile on her face and there wasn't anything I could do but push up on my tiptoes and kiss the crap out of her.

"What was that for?" she asked when I pulled away.

"Just because," I said.

Ezra went and got us a cart and followed me through the store as I picked up what I needed, throwing something in every now and then.

"You don't have to go all out for breakfast tomorrow," I said. "I promise, I'm not picky."

Reading between the lines, Ezra did not seem like much of a cook and I didn't want to put undue pressure on her to impress me with something fancy.

"What are your opinions on French toast?" she asked when we got to the bread aisle. I'd picked up some crusty bread to go with our dinner.

"Love it. Big fan," I said, and she grabbed another loaf to use for French toast, along with eggs and some maple syrup.

When we lined up at the register, I batted her hand away when she tried to put everything on the belt to pay for it all.

"I told you, you're driving."

"And the amount of gas that'll take is probably less than the price of one of these things. I've got this, Joy." She seemed really intent on paying, so I didn't fight it. I had no idea what her money situation was like, but she had a nice car and designer clothes so maybe her writing career paid well.

We paid and hauled everything to the car and then headed toward Ezra's apartment. I was dying to see it.

Ezra pulled in and we each took our share of the groceries up the stairs attached to the side of the garage. Ezra unlocked the door and pushed it open, stepping aside so I could come in and drop the heavy bags.

"Here we are," she said.

The kitchen opened right into the living room, with two doors off to my right that I assumed led to the bathroom and her bedroom. Ezra's kitchen was tiny, but it had obviously been built recently, with shiny appliances and a nice countertop with a small island that had two stools at it.

Her living room had just about enough room for a regular couch, and on the opposite wall was a built-in storage unit for the TV. On one side she had books and other knickknacks and on the other…

"Oh. Is that…?" I said, moving closer to make sure I was seeing what I thought I was seeing.

"Now you know why I don't invite a lot of people over," she said, coming to stand behind me.

I didn't have any words for a few seconds as I stared at shelf after shelf of sex toys. All kinds. Dildos, vibrators, plugs, cuffs. She even had what looked like a container for umbrellas that had several crops in it.

"I've never seen this many toys outside of a sex shop," I said.

"It's an occupational hazard," she said. "This is the majority of the things I've kept, or thought were visually pretty."

There were a number of glass pieces that looked like they wouldn't have been out of place in a museum or an art gallery.

"Joy?" Ezra asked, and I finally looked away from the toys and back at her. "What do you think?"

I took a breath. "I think that I'm not thinking about making dinner anymore."

I stepped closer to her.

"Which one is your favorite?" I asked.

"That depends on what I'm in the mood for," she said, her voice low.

I swallowed, which had become difficult.

"What mood are you in right now?" I asked and she made a groaning noise.

"The groceries are melting," she said.

"So?" I said, leaning closer to her, as if drawn by a magnet.

Ezra closed her eyes and stepped away. "You're trying to kill me, Joy."

"I'm not the one with the dildo display!" I said, gesturing. "What did you think was going to happen?"

Ezra opened her mouth and then closed it. "I guess you're right, but I wasn't going to move everything. I like them."

I snorted. This was the most unintentionally funny and arousing situation I'd ever been in.

I turned my back on the dildo display. "There. Now I can't see them. I'm still thinking about them, but I can't see them."

Ezra walked backwards into the kitchen.

"Are you going to be able to cook knowing that they're over there?" she asked as she pulled a carton of eggs out of the bag.

"I will do my best," I said.

I was not going to be able to stop thinking about them.

~

SOMEHOW, I got through making dinner without slicing my finger off or any major burns due to dildo distraction. Ezra put on a record and hummed along with it as she helped me wash and prep everything. She didn't have much in the way of cooking implements, but she had knives and a cutting board and a stove with an oven, so that was something.

To avoid spending our dinner staring at the sex toys, we sat at the island. Ezra ate a bite of the risotto and her eyes rolled back in her head.

"Oh my god, this is so good," she said, covering her mouth.

"Thanks," I said, feeling giddy from the praise. She tried

the chicken with the brussels and bacon and had a similar reaction.

"If you were trying to seduce me with food, it's working," she said as she attacked her second piece of chicken as if it was going to run away if she didn't eat it fast enough.

"I had to compete with that," I said, jerking my thumb over my shoulder. I couldn't wait to get over there and do a closer inspection on what she had. I'd have to ask her which toys were worth the money. It wasn't as if you could test drive and then return them, and she was clearly an expert. Her knowledge was valuable.

Ezra rolled her eyes. "You don't have to compete with those. Toys are enhancers. Especially when you're alone."

"I know. I mean, I'm just joking. This isn't my first experience with toys. I've got a few." I'd seen one of my favorites on her shelf, so it looked like we had similar tastes at least in that one.

"I wasn't sure. I've learned never to assume someone's history based on looking at them. I mean, if you were new to toys, I could show you the best ones to start with."

Her voice was soft, and I could see how she was going to make an incredible therapist someday. Here we were talking about sex toys and I didn't feel awkward or weird about it.

"I'm more of an intermediate than a beginner level," I said, finishing my risotto.

"Good to know," Ezra said as she took my plate and went to the dishwasher.

I packed up the leftovers and put them in the fridge. Turning around, I found Ezra right there.

"I think it's time for dessert," she said, using her body to push me up against the fridge.

"Oh?" I said, raising an eyebrow. "Do you have ice cream? Or cake? I love cake."

Ezra shook her head. "Just this." She kissed me and

tunneled her fingers through my hair, one hand taking its customary place gripping the back of my neck to angle my face up to hers. I gasped into her mouth as she used her tongue to devour me. The kiss was desperate and a little messy and I wouldn't have had it any other way.

"More," I moaned in between kisses.

"You want more?" she asked, a wicked edge to her voice.

"More," I repeated, unable to think of any others.

"You can have more. You can have whatever you want, Joy," Ezra said, and before I knew it, she had literally picked me up and carried me through the door to her bedroom. *Like a bride*, I couldn't help but think to myself before Ezra placed me on her bed. There wasn't much in the room besides a bed, a dresser, and a TV on the wall, and on the dresser more toys. The books I'd gotten her were in a stack on the nightstand.

"Oh, that reminds me. I forgot to bring you the book I picked out on Thursday," I said. I was supposed to give it to her at book club and it slipped my mind when she walked in.

"Joy. Babe. I'm not thinking about books right now," she said, her thumb brushing across my lower lip.

And just like that, I wasn't thinking about books either.

Ezra's sheets were light gray and soft, with a white comforter with dark blue checks on it. She only had two pillows, which was inconvenient, but somehow we'd make it work.

She pushed me back until she was perched above me, and I looked up into her swirling multicolored eyes.

"You're so beautiful," she said, as if in awe.

"So are you," I said. Her hair was still up, so I reached behind and pulled out the elastic as it tumbled down around us like a dark curtain. It was going to get in the way, but I didn't care. Ezra didn't usually let her hair down, that I had seen, so I was pretty happy she did with me.

Enchanted By Her

This time, Ezra didn't go slow. She kissed my mouth before sucking and licking her way down my neck.

"These clothes are getting in my way," she said, sounding disgruntled as she pulled at my shirt.

"In that case, I should probably take them off," I said, sitting up.

Ezra helped me get my shirt over my head, revealing the cute bra I had on that was white with little pink flowers and a bow right between my cleavage. My underwear had matching bows and little ribbons on the sides, but Ezra hadn't seen that yet.

"So pretty," she said, touching the bow between my boobs. I had a pretty decent set, if I said so myself. Just enough, but not too much to cause me to need a ton of support when running up the stairs. Syd's were bigger and she complained about it all the time. Her boobs had literally destroyed bras, they had that much power.

"Thanks," I said, wiggling a little bit under the intensity of her gaze.

"But not as pretty as what it's covering, I think," she said, tugging just a little bit on the bow.

Ezra helped me up so I could flick the band of my bra and pull the straps down my arms. Not sure what to do with it, I set it on the nightstand on top of the books.

I shivered a little, even though I wasn't cold.

"Look at you," Ezra said, inhaling sharply. "So pink and perfect."

I lay on my back and Ezra stared down at me with a feral look in her eye.

"Just going to look? Not going to touch?" I asked.

"Don't worry. I intend to touch with more than just my hands," she said, fluttering her fingers down the space between my boobs. My nipples puckered, as if they were begging to be touched.

"Ezra, please," I said, sounding petulant. It felt like I'd been waiting for this forever.

In response, she circled one finger around my nipple and then pinched it gently, pulling it just a tiny bit. I moaned a little and that made her smile.

Ezra cupped both my breasts in her hands and then stroked them before giving my nipples the attention they demanded. With mouth and hands, she kissed and licked and teased until my skin was damp and I was begging her for more.

It had been so long since I'd been touched and my body ached so much for it that I could barely breathe.

"Shhh, I'm going to take care of you. Don't worry," Ezra said, brushing her hand across my stomach.

I reached for the bottom of her shirt and tugged at it. I needed her skin against mine.

Ezra pulled her shirt off and I saw another basic black bra. I bet she had a whole drawer of them.

"Off please," I said, pointing to the bra.

"Bossy," she said with a grin as she pulled the bra over her head and dropped it on the floor.

At last I got to see her, including the patchwork of tattoos. I was too keyed up to study them in detail, but I was going to make her lay still later and let me catalog them all.

Her bra had covered a small tattoo between her breasts. The design looked a little bit like wings.

"I like," I said, touching it with my finger.

"Thanks," she said. I ignored the tattoos I'd already seen, the heart and the half infinity and paid attention to her other side, which bloomed with branching roses, their petals colored in with a red so dark it was like blood.

"You're so sexy," I said, running my hand down her side. Ezra's skin pebbled with goosebumps. I liked seeing her affected like I was.

"I really want to lick this right now," I said, swirling my fingers across her rib tattoo.

"You will," she said, "but right now let's get back to you."

I thought about arguing, but why would I do that? I wasn't going to turn down being worshipped by a tattooed goddess.

Ezra didn't do anything until I nodded. "Okay."

"Before I go further, let me know if there are any areas you don't like being touched, or any other boundaries you have. If I do anything to make you uncomfortable, you can just say 'stop' and I'll stop."

The intensity in Ezra's eyes was mesmerizing and I licked my lips and nodded again.

"Good," she said, stroking her hand down my neck. "And I'll do the same. Your stop is safe with me."

"Come here," I said, reaching for her. I couldn't go another moment without kissing her again. How had this incredible woman wandered into the bookstore just when I needed her? What if I hadn't asked her to be my fake wedding date? I didn't want to think about it.

"Beautiful Joy," Ezra whispered and moved down my body, giving my nipples some attention, but they were more like an appetizer. A little taste before the main course that she was heading toward.

"These have definitely got to go," Ezra said, tapping the button of my jeans. I'd purposefully worn jeans that were a little baggy on me so they'd be easier to get out of for sex purposes.

Ezra unzipped my jeans and kissed a trail down my belly and over my underwear.

"Cute," she breathed, looking up at me.

"Thanks," I said, reaching down to tangle my fingers in her hair. It was messy and her cheeks were pink and I didn't think I'd ever seen anyone as beautiful as Ezra right in this moment.

Ezra yanked my jeans down and I helped her get them off

my legs. My underwear followed soon after and there I was. Naked in Ezra's bed.

"Fuck," she breathed, sliding her hands up my thighs. "Remember when I said your smile was a gift? This is definitely like Christmas and my birthday all at once. Fuck."

I felt her hands shake just a little bit and it made me bold, seeing how much she wanted me. I wanted her too. Every cell in my body ached from it.

"I need to taste you," she said, looking down at me.

I opened my legs just a little wider. Giving her the invitation to do as she wished.

"Fuck," she said again before she slid into position between my legs and gave me one long lick that had me echoing her sentiment.

"Fuck!" I fought the urge to just steer her head by her hair, and let her set the pace.

In the past I'd had a little bit of trouble letting go when it came to sex, and it was something I had to consciously work on.

Ezra lifted one of my legs over her shoulder to open me up and put the other on my thigh.

"Joy?" she asked. She must have sensed that moment of tension.

"I'm okay. Promise," I said.

She leaned back just a little. "Do you want me to stop?"

I tightened my hold on her hair.

"Don't you dare stop, Ezra, I swear to god," I said, and she grinned.

She kissed the inside of my thigh. "Your command is my mission."

Fuck.

Ezra licked me again and I watched as she did things with her tongue that I didn't know were possible. She was going to have to demonstrate later where I could actually see what she was doing. Right now, all I could do was hold on for dear life as Ezra drove me toward an orgasm and then pulled back, then brought me to a peak, then backed off. In my head, I knew this would result in something earth-shattering, but in practice, I hated Ezra and told her so.

She just laughed and slid a finger inside me, causing my back to arch off the bed.

"Oh my god," I said as Ezra pulled her finger out almost all the way and then pumped it back inside me, curling it just a little bit to hit my G spot. My entire body seized once and I knew I was so close to coming.

"More," I said.

Ezra added another finger, flicking her tongue rapidly against my clit in an impressive display of dexterity.

"More," I moaned.

She added a third finger and ramped up the intensity with her tongue and I came apart, breaking into a thousand little sparks of light. Everything flashed bright and hot and complete as the climax tore through me, and I didn't know where it began and I ended.

At last, the rush abated and I opened my eyes to find Ezra watching me.

"You're most beautiful when you come, Joy," she said, her voice low. I wasn't so sure about that, but I was in the sparkly aftermath of an intense orgasm so I didn't care what I looked like.

"Thanks," I said, my voice coming out like mush. "You're not naked."

I pushed my lower lip out and she chuckled.

"How is it that you're getting everything you want?" she asked.

"That's not true. I almost never get what I want. Yet here you are," I said. "But if you want something, why don't you go grab whichever toy is your absolute favorite and bring it to me?"

I wasn't going to let all those toys go to waste. They deserved to be used. It was their destiny.

Ezra's eyes sparkled as she climbed off the bed and went out to the living room. She came back with the toy hidden behind her back.

"Interestingly, this was one of my first toys. This is the second one I've owned. I burned out the motor in the first one," she said, presenting me with the toy that was also one of my favorites.

"Oh, we're old friends," I said, taking the toy from her. I turned it on and listened to the familiar buzz. I was ready to go again, but I really wanted to get Ezra off.

"Take your pants off," I said, gesturing at her with the toy as if it was a magic wand. In some ways, it was.

"And here I thought you might be a little shy in the bedroom. I told you sometimes I wasn't good at reading people," she said as she slid her jeans and her underwear off in one go.

"Get that pretty tattooed ass over here," I said, banging the toy on her comforter.

Chapter Fifteen

EZRA LAY on her back next to me and we reversed positions, with me sitting up and looking down at her. I couldn't help but kiss her mouth, tasting the remnants of my desire.

The toy was set aside for now so I could get my mouth and my hands all over her skin. Especially those tattoos. I'd always been pretty neutral on them, but on Ezra? I was obsessed.

"Turn over," I said. "Just for a second."

Ezra flipped and I got a stunning view of her ass and her back, which was covered in bright, beautiful tattoos.

"Gorgeous," I said, running my hand down her spine. She looked over her shoulder at me.

"Now let me lick your nipples," I said.

"You are a bossy one," she said. "Unexpected, but a welcome surprise."

Ezra turned over again and I gathered her breasts in my hands before lowering my head to take one of her nipples into my mouth.

For some reason, I thought about the ridiculous phrase "candy nipples" and couldn't help but laugh.

"What is it?" Ezra asked and I looked up at her though my lashes.

"You have candy nipples," I said, and she snorted, one of her hands running through my hair.

"I think that's the nicest thing anyone's ever said about my nipples," she said.

"You're welcome."

I focused on my task to show her just how much I appreciated her body. Everything about her turned me on so much that I was so ready to come again, it would only take sneaking my hand between my legs or rubbing myself against her to set me off.

My tongue and lips made their way down her body and I was going to taste her before I got my hands on the toy, since I couldn't do both at the same time without buzzing my face off.

Before I touched her with my tongue, I looked up at her, finding her watching me with unwavering intensity.

"How flexible are you?" I asked.

Ezra smirked at me and put her hands on the insides of her thighs, pulling them apart until she was completely open for me.

"Fuck me," I said, and Ezra let out a sexy giggle.

"Yoga and Pilates," she said. "And bendy joints, I guess."

I barely heard her over all the blood rushing right from my brain to other areas of my body.

"You are the sexiest person I've ever met, and I can't believe this is real right now," I said, taking one finger and drawing it through her center. She was already wet and glistening even without my mouth.

"Joy, please," Ezra said, and I noticed that her legs were trembling, shaking the mattress just a little bit.

"What do you want?" I asked, deciding to mess with her a little bit.

"Stick out your tongue," she said, her voice needy.

Weird request, but okay. I did.

"I want that," she said pointing, "on this." She pointed to her pussy. "*Now.*"

Shiiitttttt. This woman was going to kill me.

"You got it, babe," I said, and instead of licking her I circled her clit with my tongue before licking straight up and down and doing another circle.

I learned Ezra with my tongue and my ears and by touch. I heard her breath quicken and felt her fingers in my hair and explored her heated skin, looking for just the right place, just the right pressure that would give her what she needed.

"Babe, I'm so close," she said as I sucked on the side of her clit, tilting my head to get the right angle.

I coated my hand in her arousal and slid one finger inside her as she gasped.

"I'm so close, fuck me with two or three fingers," she said. This was a woman who knew what she wanted and needed.

I immediately drove two fingers inside her, making sure she was ready before adding a third, since my hands were relatively small. She hadn't asked for a fourth, but it could definitely fit, but we could save that for next time. I had no intention of this being the only time I gave her an orgasm tonight. My new goal was to try out every single one of those toys with her.

I curled my fingers to hit that special place inside her at the same time as I sucked hard on the side of her clit and I felt her start to come as her legs drew in, nearly clamping around my ears.

The first time she came hadn't been an anomaly. Ezra was loud, and I'd never heard my name said so many times while making a woman climax. It was my new favorite thing.

At last her body stopped shuddering and her legs fell to the mattress beside me and she looked down at me with a smile.

"You're incredible," she said with a little gasp as she was hit with an aftershock.

"I do what I can, babe," I said, kissing the insides of both her thighs before crawling up to lay next to her.

"I didn't use the toy. I was having too much fun," I said, wiping my face. Both of us were a mess, and we'd made a disaster of the bed too.

"It's okay," she said, putting her arm around me and pulling me in to lay on her sweaty chest, "we can use it later."

~

EZRA and I snuggled a little until I needed to kiss her again and that led to her turning the tables and using the toy on me to earth-shattering results. Not to be outdone, I attacked her and got her to scream in record time.

"And that's how it's done," I said, holding up the toy and blowing on it, as if it were a smoking gun.

"You're adorable when you're smug," she said, taking the toy from me and setting it on the nightstand. She held me again until the comforter was too uncomfortable to lay on and we got up to take a quick shower and change the bed. Ezra also got out some waterproof pads to lay over the bed.

"Wow, this is a whole other level," I said.

"I can get messy sometimes. *Really* messy," she said with a wink.

"*Oh*," I said, understanding her meaning. "Well that I have to see."

She ripped the towel from my body and grabbed me, kissing me hard.

"You definitely will."

~

BY THE TIME the sky started turning lighter with the arrival of dawn, we had a pile of toys that needed cleaning, and both our bodies were loose and completely exhausted. I was also starving.

"I came up with a better term for dry humping, at least for the two of us," Ezra said through a yawn. Our limbs were tangled together, and I knew we should probably get some sleep, but I didn't want to close my eyes.

"What's that?" I asked.

She smiled down at me. "Clam slamming."

I burst out laughing and couldn't stop. Tears streamed from my eyes as Ezra joined in my laughter.

"I thought it was good."

"No, it's good," I said, wiping my eyes. "A little violent, but it works."

Ezra kissed my forehead. "We should get some sleep."

I sighed. "Okay." I couldn't fight anymore and finally passed out, still laughing about clam slamming.

∼

"BABE. Joy. We need to get up," Ezra said, touching my shoulder. It was early afternoon, and I definitely hadn't gotten enough sleep. Ezra wore a tank top and a pair of gray boyshorts and her hair was up in a messy bun.

"I'm up," I said, my voice rusty from lack of sleep.

"Do you want some coffee? I've got the French toast almost ready too."

I grabbed her shirt and pulled her mouth down for a quick kiss.

"You're the actual best, you know that."

She grinned and turned around to go back to the kitchen. I dove out of bed to smack her ass before she walked away.

∼

WE ATE breakfast and downed as much coffee as we could before getting dressed in our shower clothes. My hair was a little weird from sleeping with it wet, so I did a quick braid.

"Is this okay?" Ezra asked, showing me her outfit.

Today she'd abandoned her usual flannel and dark colors for a white sleeveless shirt paired with a dark blue blazer and black pants. She hadn't ditched her signature leather boots, though, which I was glad to see.

"You look incredible," I said, wanting to throw her back into bed and clasping my hands behind my back so I didn't.

"Thanks," she said. "Do you need a hand?"

I'd been struggling to zip the back of my dark-brown dress up.

"I'd love one," I said, turning my back so that Ezra could zip the dress up. She placed a kiss on the back of my neck after she finished.

"There," she said. "Beautiful."

I turned around and then checked myself out in Ezra's bathroom mirror. I'd brought a little bit of makeup with me, so I did a quick layer of tinted moisturizer, some blush, mascara, and lip stain. Most days I didn't wear a ton of makeup, but I figured since a lot of pictures would be taken and I looked like I hadn't slept, it couldn't hurt. I also dotted some concealer under my eyes to make me look more awake.

"Stunning," Ezra said, pulling me in for a kiss. "Ready?"

I made sure I had my gift, a set of fancy towels which had been ordered from Anna's registry.

As we were heading for the door, I remembered something else.

"Wait!" I said, pulling out my phone. "I forgot I need to send you money."

Ezra stared at me.

"I'm so sorry, give me just a sec," I said, pulling up my payment app.

"You're not sending me money," Ezra said.

"No, we agreed," I said, filling out the amount. I was just about to send it when she snatched the phone out of my hand.

"You're not paying me, Joy," she said, her voice firm.

"But we agreed," I said, reaching for my phone.

"You're not paying me," she said again.

If we didn't leave now, we were going to be late. "We'll talk about it later," I said, hoping that would end the matter for now.

Ezra handed my phone back and I closed the app without paying her.

"If you send it to me, I'm going to send it right back," she said as we got in the car.

"Okay, okay," I said, unable to understand why she was suddenly being weird about this. Sure, we were seeing each other, but this wedding ordeal was part of our original deal.

Ezra was mostly silent as we drove to Emily's house in Redfield, where the shower would be held. Since my parents had downsized, Emily had the largest place to host, with a full finished basement and lots of parking. She kind of lived in the middle of nowhere, but her house was really nice, so it was a trade-off.

Ezra pulled in behind a row of cars already here and we rushed to the entrance to the basement, which was covered in balloons and a sign.

I pushed through the door and was hit with the noise of a bunch of people crammed in a room together.

Jill, Anna's best friend and maid of honor, greeted us at the door. I gave her a hug and introduced Ezra. She showed me where the food and gift tables were and said that Anna had banned games and public opening of gifts.

"How did that go over with my mom?" My other two sister's showers had been multi-hour ordeals and I'd just barely survived.

Jill's smile was rueful. "Not well. I think Faith and Emily are in charge of making sure she doesn't get on a chair and announce one anyway. The only thing Anna would allow is if you want to fill out a card with some advice for her upcoming marriage, you can do that. Oh, and don't forget to sign the guestbook."

Jill moved on to welcome another group of guests, so Ezra followed me to the gift table, which was covered in a tablecloth and silk leaves. Garlands of more silk leaves draped the walls, along with the same ring balloons I'd used at book club.

"I should say hello to Anna," I said, looking around and finding her in a corner with Mom, Faith, and Emily.

"Oh no," I said. "This might get ugly."

Ezra followed me again as I worked my way through the crowd, saying hello to people I knew.

By the time I got to my family, it looked like Faith and Emily had pulled Mom away from Anna.

"Hey," I said, giving her a hug. "Everything okay?"

Anna closed her eyes and took a deep breath. She wore a white dress with a simple burnt orange belt as a nod to the fall theme.

"Mom was trying to instigate games again," she said.

"I'm sorry." I rubbed her arm. She was practically vibrating with stress. "Do you want to go get a drink or something to eat?" I had the suspicion that she hadn't eaten yet today.

She nodded and I brought her over to the table and pushed a plate into her hands.

"You look gorgeous," I said.

"Thanks," she said. "I can't believe it's happening so soon. Feels like just yesterday we got engaged."

I got her to eat and my sisters calmed my mom down and everything seemed fine after that, except for Ezra. She stayed with me and chatted politely, but that wall had gone up between us again and I didn't like it.

"Are you okay?" I asked after we'd both signed the guest book.

She nodded and gave me a tight smile, which really bugged me.

"Come on," I said, taking her hand and leading her out the door.

It was chilly outside, but it wasn't too cold. To give us some privacy, I towed her to the car and got in, waiting for her. She sat in the driver's seat and shut the door. I faced her.

"What's going on?" I asked. "You've been weird since I mentioned paying. I know we said we'd talk about it later, but I can't deal with you shutting me out. What's going on?" I asked, breathing a little heavily. Being confrontational was still completely terrifying for me, but I couldn't take the silence for another second.

Ezra opened her mouth and then closed it. She took a breath.

"I don't want you to pay me because I love you," she finally said and I sat there and stared at her.

"Can you repeat that?"

"I love you," Ezra said. "I...I don't know how it happened, but I came in this morning and saw you sleeping in my bed and realized I didn't want to let you go. Ever. And I didn't want to be your paid wedding date. I wanted to be yours, in every way."

I gaped at her, completely thrown by this turn of events.

"You love me?" I asked. "And that's why you've been weird today?"

Ezra chuckled softly. "Basically."

"Oh," I said. "That's a lot to process."

"I didn't intend to tell you like this. It's still so new that I wasn't going to do anything about it, but then you dragged me to the car and here we are." She gave me a nervous smile and then silence fell between us for a few seconds.

"You don't have to say anything," she said. "I'm not expecting you to say anything. I know it's fast. I know it doesn't make sense." She was babbling a little and it was so adorable I wanted to kiss her.

My irritation at Ezra had completely melted away, leaving something much more all-consuming and powerful in its wake.

Love.

Pure, clear, unconditional love.

I loved this woman who put up with my wacky family and loved books and had a sex toy collection to rival a museum. She was kind and she made me laugh and made every day better since she'd walked into the bookstore and agreed to be my fake wedding date.

"Joy?" Ezra asked, her hand rhythmically tapping on the shifter knob.

The words fell out of my mouth before I could stop them. "I love you."

Now she was the shocked one. "What?"

"I love you too, and I'm not just saying it because you said it. In some ways I think I fell a little bit in love with you the second I first saw you," I said, and the truth of those words shook me to my core. Something in me had known from that first meeting that Ezra was going to change my life, but I'd had no idea by how much.

"Joy," she said, her voice soft as she reached out and stroked my face. "What the fuck is going on?" She laughed and I laughed and then I was laughing and crying at the same time with the absurdity of it all.

"Come here," she said, and we were kissing in a car again, only this time there was no coffee to spill.

Ezra kissed me and even though it was uncomfortable kissing in a car, it didn't matter. Everything about this moment was right and perfect and just the way it was supposed to be.

She pulled back and pressed her forehead to mine, her face so close it was blurry.

"I love you," she said softly. "I couldn't help myself."

"I guess I'm pretty lovable," I said, laughing. "I still can't believe this is real."

"I'm real. You're real. This is real." She held my face between her hands and kissed me again.

"Now you're stuck with me and my family," I said.

"I think I'll find some way to deal with it," she said. "As long as I get you."

"I'm yours," I said.

∽

THE TWO OF us made out in the car for a while, and eventually went back to the party to have some cake, pack up a slice for Syd, and then head back to Ezra's so I could show her just how much I loved her.

We stumbled to the bedroom, yanking at zippers and shirts and shoes as we fell into bed.

"I love you," I said, smiling up at her.

"I love you, Joy," she said as she slid her hand inside my underwear to find me wet and ready for her.

"Oh, fuck, babe," she said, and I couldn't help myself from doing the same as we rolled to the side, each fucking the other with our fingers as we kissed.

I came first, with Ezra following right after me.

I panted and stared at her as she came down and I brought my hand to my mouth to lick my fingers.

Ezra nuzzled my nose with hers and held me close.

"I thought loving you was going to be completely terrifying and it is, but not in the way I thought it was going to be," she said, taking the elastic out of my braid. I did the same to her, running my damp fingers through the strands, so happy just to be with her and touch her.

"Love can be scary," I said. "But without it, what's the point?"

Ezra smiled. "You're right. I've been on my own for so long, but I don't want to be like that anymore. Ever since I first came to Arrowbridge, it felt like a place I could stay. I couldn't explain the feeling, but being here feels right. Being here feels like home," she said.

"Stay home with me," I said.

"I'd love to," she said, kissing me again.

～

WE SPENT the rest of the evening together and I sent Sydney a message that I was going to spend the rest of the weekend with Ezra.

I KNEW IT she responded and demanded a dish session when I came back to the apartment. I promised I'd give her details (not all of them, obviously) on Monday when we had lunch together.

"Do you want to go grab some clothes? You're also welcome to anything of mine," Ezra said. We were still in bed, but my stomach had started grumbling.

"I'll just wear your clothes," I said. Then I'd get to smell like her.

Ezra gave me a baggy flannel shirt and some shorts that I wore as she rummaged around in the fridge. We had leftovers from dinner the night before, so she heated them up and we ate them on the couch, our legs propped up on the coffee table.

"We went through a lot of your collection last night," I said. "I'm pretty impressed."

"Me too. But there are still a lot of things to try," she said, her eyes twinkling.

"We should make a spreadsheet," I said. "I could reformat my reading log."

Ezra snorted and pulled me in for a kiss.

"What was that for?" I asked.

"You. Just being you."

I set my plate down and crawled into her lap, forgetting all about dinner.

Chapter Sixteen

Ezra and I spent the rest of Saturday and Sunday in a haze of sex. She dropped me off, sore and sated, on Sunday night so I could get some sleep and be ready for work on Monday.

"I thought this weekend was going to go one way and it went in a completely different direction," I said, kissing her goodbye as she pressed me up against the passenger door of her car.

"A good direction?" she asked.

"The best direction," I said. "You'll be over for dinner tomorrow night?"

I couldn't believe I was going back to my own bed to sleep alone. This weekend had changed absolutely everything about my life.

"I'll drop into the bookstore too. Bring you an afternoon coffee."

"Oh my god, that sounds wonderful. You're wonderful," I said.

Ezra laughed and pulled me in for a tight hug. That wall she'd thrown up between us when we'd first met was gone and she was just my warm, open Ezra. Mine.

"I'm sure Sydney is standing in front of the door waiting to hear everything," she said as she pulled back, but kept her arms around me.

"I know. She's going to want to hear everything, and I mean everything, but some things are just for you and me," I said.

"You and me is my favorite thing," she said.

"Mine too."

∽

SYDNEY WAS WAITING with a glass of wine and a gleam in her eye.

"I swear to god, you have to give me enough details," she said, shoving the glass into my hand and then dragging me to the couch.

I laughed and sat down with her.

"Well, we went to the grocery store—" I started to say, but Sydney interrupted me.

"I don't give a fuck about that. Tell me everything important."

I had been trying to mess with her a little bit, but I was bursting to tell her how much things had changed with Ezra.

"She said she loves me," I said.

"What?!" Sydney shrieked, spilling her entire glass of wine all over the couch and ignoring it as she grabbed my arm, almost spilling mine. I set it out of the way so she didn't upend that one too.

"She said she loves me and I said I loved her. It was unbelievable, Syd."

I sat with my best friend on the couch and told her all the (non-salacious) details and she held my hand and smiled and hugged me.

"I knew it. I knew it! I told you that she was going to be the one. You're welcome."

I giggled, feeling drunk even though I hadn't had any of my wine.

"I can't believe it happened, honestly. It feels like a dream."

"I can tell. You're basically floating right now."

I couldn't stop laughing as Sydney went to the kitchen to grab a sponge to deal with the wine on the couch.

"I'm so happy for you," she said, scrubbing at the couch with a little too much force.

"Thanks," I said, hoping she was telling the truth.

"Plus, now you don't have to pay her the other six hundred bucks, so it was a budget-friendly idea to fall in love with her."

I snorted.

"I hadn't thought about it that way."

Sydney kept scrubbing until I took the sponge from her.

"Are you okay?" I asked.

She smiled. "Absolutely. I'm just happy for you." She gave me a hug, but I didn't really believe her. I decided to drop it for now, since it was getting late, and I was completely exhausted from all the sex.

"So," Syd said, dropping the sponge on the coffee table. "Tell me about the sex."

I threw a pillow at her.

EZRA MESSAGED me the next morning and couldn't stop smiling as I unlocked the bookstore.

"Good morning," I sang to Kendra.

"Whoa, you are beaming. Have a good weekend?"

"Pretty much the best weekend ever."

I filled her in on Ezra and she gave me a hug.

"I knew you two were meant for each other. Sometimes you can just see it," she said as we opened for the day.

I did my best to focus on my job, but I couldn't wait to see Ezra. She sent me messages throughout the morning and I sent some back. I had to keep putting my phone away so I didn't spend all my working hours messaging her and get myself fired.

Sydney seemed normal during lunch, grumbling about her job and asking how Ezra was, so I didn't say anything about her being a little off the night before.

It had crossed my mind that Syd might be a little jealous, or worried that things were going to change between us now that I was with Ezra. We definitely saw Layne less now that she was with Honor. I wasn't going to let my relationship with Ezra completely take over my life. My friendships were just as important to me. I sent Layne a message filling her in and she said she'd already heard a lot from Syd.

We need to have a girl's night. THIS WEEK she sent, and I said I'd talk to Syd and we could schedule it.

Ezra came in at two, which was right before the after-school rush.

"Caramel macchiato," she said, presenting me with the cup.

"Get out of here," Kendra said, pushing me toward the stock room. "Don't be too long."

"I won't," I promised her and headed for the stock room, Ezra right behind me. I set the coffee down and closed the door, kissing her like we'd been apart for years.

"I missed you," I said.

"I know, I missed you," she said. "But if we keep kissing, then I'm going to end up fucking you in here and then you might get fired and I know you love this job."

I groaned and stepped away from her. "You're right."

She handed me my coffee and we both sat down, our chairs with a little bit of distance between them.

"How would you like to go on a date with me this week?" she asked.

"A real date?" I asked and she nodded.

It seemed a little bit backwards that we said we'd loved each other even before our first real date, but it didn't matter. We'd done things in our own order.

"Maybe I can take you back to that bar in Castleton. Have a do-over."

"Ohhh, I'm going to order an Ezrarita," I said, teasing her.

"We're not calling it that. I've decided that it should be called a Candy Nipple," she said with a straight face.

I almost spit out my coffee. "Okay, okay, we can call it Candy Nipple."

"Good," she said, scooting her chair closer to me. "We'll drink Candy Nipples and if it's karaoke night, maybe I'll get up and sing."

I set my coffee aside and leaned toward her. "Only if I get to pick the song."

"Deal," she said just before our lips met.

Epilogue

"Come dance with me," I said, taking Ezra's hand and pulling her toward the dance floor.

Anna and Robert's wedding had, so far, gone off without a hitch. Mom had cried through the whole ceremony and hadn't criticized Anna once.

Ezra looked utterly mouthwatering in her suit, and I was determined to show her just how sexy she looked when we got back to her place later.

These past few weeks with her had been unbelievable. She'd slid right into my life and my world as if she'd always been there. Ezra and Syd even had formed a friendship that made my heart swell every time I caught them laughing together.

Things with Ezra had gone fast, and I had the feeling that pretty soon she was going to ask me to move in with her. It made sense, since I spent more than half my time at her place.

We swayed on the dance floor together and nothing could interrupt the moment except for my phone vibrating in Ezra's pocket. I'd given it to her to carry during the ceremony.

She fished it out and handed it to me. It was from Sydney.

I did something bad last night she sent.

I frowned at the message. This could mean anything. I was going to need some more details.

What do you mean? I asked.

"What's going on?" Ezra asked.

"Syd said she did something bad last night. I have no idea what that means. Could be anything." It could mean she over-plucked her eyebrows or set fire to the apartment and anything in between.

Forget it. You're at the wedding. We can talk about it later. Have a good time! Her response was all over the place.

Are you sure everything is okay? Do you need me to leave? I sent, trying not to worry.

No, I promise I'm fine. Just being dramatic. Have a great time with Ezra. Bring me some cake? She responded.

"She says it's no big deal and asked if I could bring cake. I guess she's okay," I said.

"Do you want to call her just to make sure?" Ezra asked as we walked off the floor.

"Yeah, just to check."

I called Syd and she picked up right away.

"Hey, are you sure you're okay?" I asked.

"Yeah, yeah, I'm fine. Promise," she said, and I swore I could hear another voice in the background.

"Is someone there with you? Joy, did you hook up with someone last night?"

"What? No. I mean, maybe. We'll talk later." There was definitely someone there with her.

I rolled my eyes at Ezra. "She hooked up and whoever it is is still there. No emergency," I said, giving my phone back to her. "Let's go, my sexy date," I said, towing her back onto the dance floor.

Ezra danced for longer than I thought she would, and I was shocked to see her dancing and laughing with my sisters. She'd won them over, and had even charmed my mom. Dad had been enamored of her from that first dinner. Everyone loved Ezra.

She pulled me close for a slow song and I let myself melt into her arms.

"I'm really glad I agreed to be your fake wedding date," she said. I pulled back so I could look into her eyes.

"I'm really glad I was so overwhelmed by your hotness that I asked you."

She threw her head back and laughed.

"I love you," she said.

"I love you, Ezra Evans."

THANKS SO FOR READING! **Reviews are SO appreciated!** They can be long or short, or even just a star rating.

READ THE NEXT BOOK, Tempted By Her, where Sydney's one-night stand ends up becoming her roommate and keeping her hands to herself becomes a bigger challenge than she anticipated...

Turn the page to read the first chapter!

About Tempted By Her

I wasn't looking forward to finding a new roommate after my best friend, Joy, moved in with her girlfriend, Ezra. We've lived together for years, and I didn't want to start over with a stranger. Then there's a fire at the house Lark's renting and for some reason I open my mouth and offer to let her move in with me.

Lark Conroy, the same woman I had one blisteringly hot night with months ago and have pretended to be normal around ever since. When it comes to love, I'm allergic to romance. I like to hit-it and quit-it and move on with my life.

There's no reason I can't be cordial and normal with Lark while we live together temporarily. We're both mature adults. Well, I'm not that mature, but I can fake it.

Turns out pretending I don't want to kiss Lark every waking moment is harder than I thought, and spending time with her is giving me feelings that I've never had before and don't know what to do with. I'm in a situation and I have absolutely no idea how to stop myself from falling in love with her, or if I even want to.

I didn't intended to fuck Lark Conroy, it kind of just happened. I would have blamed alcohol, except I'd been completely sober.

After a disastrous meeting with a potential hookup that turned out to be a married couple looking for a third, I'd decided to go on a sexual hiatus for a little while. Having fun with hookups had been my thing for years, and I decided I needed a break.

It had nothing to do with the fact that my two best friends had fallen in love. I was just going on hiatus for a little while.

Focus on myself. Meditate and shit. Whatever.

It wasn't like I wasn't getting off. I was just not getting off with other people to help. My hand and my favorite vibrator were my partners.

Everything was going fine, or at least sort of fine. I was grouchy and having issues sleeping and blowing my cool at work, but I was adjusting. Joy, my best friend, would usually distract me and hug me and bake me something to make me feel better, but she was completely in love with Ezra, the woman she paid to be her wedding date to her sister's wedding. Weird, but who was I to judge?

Left to my own devices, I didn't make the best decisions.

Decisions that led me to end up at a random bar in a random town on a random Friday night. Joy was off with Ezra, and I wouldn't even see her until Monday since they were headed to her sister's wedding.

I'd just needed to get out of Arrowbridge for a bit. Growing up there and then living as an adult in the same town gave me sympathy for goldfish in clear bowls, with everyone watching them and seeing their business.

The bar was dim and a little grungy, which was how bars should be, in my opinion. There was also a grizzled dude wearing flannel sitting at the end of the bar nursing a beer, which a good bar should also have.

The bartender was one of those women who could be thirty or seventy and you couldn't really tell in the low light.

Since I was driving myself, I figured it was best to say sober. One drink would lead to two and that would lead to me potentially being a dumbass.

"Just a Coke with lime, please," I said, and the bartender gave me a disapproving look, but she made the drink and shoved it at me.

"Hi, can I get a rum runner?" a voice said next to me. I thought it sounded familiar, so I turned to find Lark Conroy leaning against the bar next to me.

"Hey," I said, and it took her a second to place me.

"Oh, hey. Sydney, right?"

She and I had met a few times, since she was the sister of Layne's girlfriend, Honor, but I'd never really talked to her.

"Yeah," I said as the bartender handed Lark her drink with a little more courtesy than she'd shown to mine.

"Do you mind?" Lark asked, pointing to the empty stool next to me. My intention had been to wallow in my misery in this bar alone, but something about the way the light hit her blonde hair and the way her blue eyes looked in the dark made me say, "Not at all."

It was no secret that Lark was gorgeous. Not in that polished and perfect way her sister, Honor was. Whereas Honor was designer perfume and stilettos, Lark was messy waves and ripped jeans. Lark was pretty in the way that you imagined what she'd look like in your bed.

I closed my eyes for a second to try and stop that runaway train of thoughts. It didn't lead anywhere good.

"What brings you here?" she asked, and I decided that a little small talk wouldn't hurt anyone.

"Just out wandering. I got sick of Arrowbridge," I said, sipping my drink and wishing it had alcohol in it.

"You grew up there, right?" she asked and I was surprised

she remembered.

"Yup," I said with a sigh.

"Sounds rough," she said, tilting her body toward me.

"It can be. What are you doing so far from Castelton?" I asked.

She shrugged. "Had to get away."

"Too many chickens?" I asked and she smiled, making my body zing with awareness of just how pretty she was.

"I keep having nightmares about them murdering me by pecking me to death." I laughed.

Lark's rental was a tiny little house owned by an elderly woman with a chicken fetish, I was convinced. Chickens on the rugs, chickens on the walls, chicken tchotchkes on every available surface. Excessive was an understatement.

"Maybe it's time to move," I said.

She sighed and sipped aggressively at her drink.

"I would, but I'm pretty much broke. I'm sure Layne has told you about my situation," she said, frowning.

"I mean, I know you're working part time and you took a break from school," I said carefully. I didn't want her to feel shitty about her life. I had no room to judge. I'd barely, and I mean barely, gotten a business degree only to come back home broke to manage my mom's pottery studio, which I could have done even without the degree.

"You can say I dropped out," she said, rolling her eyes.

"If you were just wasting money and it wasn't going toward anything, then dropping out was just smart," I said.

She leaned her elbow against the bar and leaned her head on it.

"You think so?"

There was a twinkle in her eyes that that only spelled trouble. With a capital T.

"I do," I said, leaning closer.

Find out what happens next…

Afterword

Like this book? Read Just One Night and meet the Castleton Crew where the beach days are hot and the romance is hotter!

Sign up for my newsletter and gain access to free books, bonus chapters, short stories, news, and more!

Reading List

This is How You Lose the Time War by Amal El-Mohtar and Max Gladstone (Chapter 7)

D'Vaughn and Kris Plan a Wedding by Chencia C. Higgins (Chapter 8)

She Who Became the Sun by Shelley Parker-Chan (Chapter 13)

Knit One, Girl Two by Shira Glassman (Chapter 13)

About the Author

Chelsea M. Cameron is a New York Times/USA Today/Internationally Best Selling author from Maine who now lives and works in Boston. She's a red velvet cake enthusiast, obsessive tea drinker, former cheerleader, and world's worst video gamer. When not writing, she enjoys watching infomercials, eating brunch in bed, tweeting, and playing fetch with her cat, Sassenach. She has a degree in journalism from the University of Maine, Orono that she promptly abandoned to write about the people in her own head. More often than not, these people turn out to be just as weird as she is.

Connect with her on Twitter, Facebook, Instagram, Bookbub, Goodreads, and her Website.

If you liked this book, please take a few moments to **leave a review**. Authors really appreciate this and it helps new readers find books they might enjoy. Thank you!

Also by Chelsea M. Cameron

The Noctalis Chronicles
Fall and Rise Series
My Favorite Mistake Series
The Surrender Saga
Rules of Love Series
UnWritten
Behind Your Back Series
OTP Series
Brooks (The Benson Brothers)
The Violet Hill Series
Unveiled Attraction
Anyone but You
Didn't Stay in Vegas
Wicked Sweet
Christmas Inn Maine
Bring Her On
The Girl Next Door
Who We Could Be
Castleton Hearts

Enchanted By Her is a work of fiction. Names, characters, places and incidents are either the product of the author's imagination or are use fictitiously. Any resemblance to actual persons, living or dead, events, business establishments or locales is entirely coincidental.

No part of this book may be reproduced, scanned or distributed in any printed or electronic form without permission. All rights reserved.

Copyright © 2022 Chelsea M. Cameron

Editing by Laura Helseth

Cover by Chelsea M. Cameron

Printed in Great Britain
by Amazon